Oblivious

LESLIE MCADAM

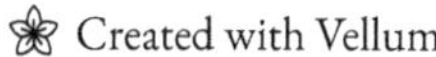 Created with Vellum

My hot best friend has no idea what he's doing to me.

He sends me naughty texts at the most inappropriate times. He lets me fall asleep on top of him when we watch movies. And his protective side comes out if I dance too close to anyone at our favorite club.

Correct me if I'm wrong, but those are things a *boyfriend* does. Except August isn't my boyfriend, he's my *best* friend, and those lines are drawn in permanent marker. The one time we tried to cross the boundary between friends and lovers, it failed so spectacularly that we never did it again. So ... "friends" is good enough. That's what I tell myself. Because at least I have him in my life. Without him, I'd be lost.

But after we're dared to kiss, and that kiss reshapes reality, we agree to be friends who do things with each other. Nakey things.

That makes my life so much better. And so much worse. After

all, August doesn't want to settle down, and he never wants to get married. While I do.

Most importantly, no matter how our relationship changes, he can't find out I'm desperately in love with him.

Oblivious *is a sweet and steamy contemporary m/m romance about best friends who don't know they're already dating. Noah and August are always touching, finish each other's sentences, and bristle whenever the other gets within six feet of a date, but they can't see what's crystal clear to everyone else.* Oblivious *features badly timed sexy texts, a hot kiss that rocks two men's universes, and (unofficially, but likely) the highest number of heartfelt marriage proposals in a romance novel ever.*

Before we get started, I want to acknowledge the brave people throughout history who have fought very hard for the right to be free from sexual harassment. The manner in which August and I behave is absolutely a case of "the cobbler's kids have no shoes." In this instance, the lawyer does things that are illeg—

No. I'm not admitting anything.

Let's just say that if any of my clients hypothetically were to do what we do, like texting explicit sexual content during the workday (much less things I only dream about, like having sex with my best friend on his desk … or mine), I'd be telling them to stop, and there'd be a letter from me to them in the file documenting that they went against my advice when they later got sued for creating a hostile work environment. The fact that August and I believe what we're doing doesn't hurt anyone doesn't make it true, and I understand if laughing about playing sexy games in the office is offensive because of your real-world experiences. I don't want to minimize those in any way but rather create a safe place to experience some fantasies—between the pages of a book.

Oh, and August also gets me to smoke pot. Sometimes. Okay, maybe more than sometimes.

But California legalized it.

Gosh, those sound like excuses. Anyway, if either of those topics is not something you want to read about, this isn't the book for you.

And, I might add, if you're looking for something dark and full of angst, that isn't this book either.

* * *

Additional content warning: includes themes and portrayal of abandonment by a parent, death of a sibling (referenced only), dementia, injuries and hospital scenes, plus swearing, explicit sex, and alcohol use.

Prologue

AUGUST

Age nine

I peer out the front window at the street. A U-Haul truck idles at the curb in front of our neighbor's house, and boxes are stacked on the sidewalk next to furniture.

"Is Mr. Weston moving away?" I ask my mom, who's braiding my younger sister May's long, dark, curly hair with deft fingers. May fidgets—she's three—and my mother shushes her, then kisses her cheek. My mom's always dressed pretty nice and wears makeup, so her kiss leaves a lipstick print on May's face. May wipes at it but lets my mom finish.

"No, he's not moving out. His grandson's coming to live with him. Moving from Woodland Hills, I think?" We live in Burbank on a street with lots of trees.

I furrow my brows and set down my game controller. "How old is he?" I demand, putting my hand on my hip.

Mom smiles, shoos May away, and stands up to squeeze my shoulder before picking up April, the baby, who's one. "I think he's your age. When I saw Harvey at the mailbox last week, he mentioned his grandson was coming to stay. I didn't know when that was going to happen, but I guess it's to—"

Before she finishes her sentence, I'm outside and skidding to a stop next door.

If the new kid's even halfway cool, I'll be so happy. I'm sick of being the oldest and the only boy in a family of girls. None of my cousins is my age, either. I want a friend who's my age.

The sun is bright in my eyes as I check out the kid in front of me, who's just emerged from the house.

He's small, with huge blue eyes and curly blond hair, and he looks like he's near tears. Mr. Weston is crouched in front of him, talking to him earnestly. When the kid notices me, he quickly wipes his eyes with the backs of his hands and then blinks rapidly like I won't figure out that he's been crying.

I grin, shoving my hands in my pockets. "Hey, I'm August. August Ramirez."

"Noah Weston," he says, shifting his weight from one foot to the other.

Mr. Weston smiles at me, although it seems kind of strained. Then he tells Noah, "I told you the neighbors had a boy your age you could play with."

"Are you moving in?" I ask. "That's what my mom said."

"Yeah. My mom ..." He bites his lip.

A shadow passes across Mr. Weston's face. "His mom thought it best if Noah stays with us for a while."

I don't understand what's happening, but it feels like Noah's mom is being mean. My mom would never ship us off to live with our grandma. We love Abuelita, but she isn't my mom.

"Can I help with something?" I ask. "I could move boxes."

Again, Mr. Weston's smile is tight. "We don't need help, but Noah might want company. Isn't that right, bud?"

Noah shrugs, and I decide that he's my new friend.

"I'll show you Noah's room," a woman says from behind us. I turn and see Mrs. Weston, Noah's grandma, standing on the front porch. "We cleared out a space in the guest bedroom and brought his bed and dresser so he'd feel more at home."

"Want me to help you set up?" I ask, throwing an arm around Noah.

He stiffens for a moment, then nods.

I step back. "Sorry. We touch a lot in my family. I forget not everyone is like that."

"That's okay. I'm, uh, good with it."

"Cool."

I follow them into the small, tidy house that smells like lemon Pledge and is full of old-fashioned furniture. It's pretty much like mine, except only two—now three—people live in it, instead of the seven of us (my parents, my four sisters, and me) plus whoever else feels like hanging out, which is normally my mom's three sisters and Tío Raymond.

Mrs. Weston leads us down the hall to a small bedroom that contains, in addition to the bed and dresser, an empty bookshelf and piles of boxes. I look around. "This is so cool. You have your own room."

Noah stares at me.

"I have to share everything with my sisters. They're pains in the rear. Especially Juli. She's seven and takes my stuff."

Mr. Weston continues to bring boxes in while I work with Noah to set up his PlayStation. When Mr. Weston says he's going to go return the U-Haul, Mrs. Weston stays home with us. She makes the bed and puts Noah's clothes away, and I help him place his books on his shelves. I bet it's hard being in a different place.

But he's got me. I'll show him the ropes.

"Why did your mom want you to stay here?" I ask, as Noah hands me the last of his comics.

He looks away. "She has other things going on. She's moving in with her boyfriend."

I frown. "And you can't go?"

"She said there's not enough room for all of us."

That doesn't sound right to me, but I can tell he doesn't want to talk about it anymore. So instead, we arrange his LEGOs on the shelf. He has some big ones, like the *Millennium Falcon*. When we're done setting up his room, I grin at him. "I'm glad you're my neighbor."

Noah's look of relief is palpable. "Yeah?"

I nod. "Do you want to go for a bike ride after dinner?"

"I don't have a bike," he mutters.

"You can borrow one of ours."

He shrugs. "Okay."

I want to invite him for dinner, but Mrs. Weston says that she and Mr. Weston want to have him to themselves for a moment. She says yes to bike riding after dinner, though. I ask if he can come for dinner tomorrow, and she says, "We'll see." I think that means yes.

With a wave, I head back to my house, a happy feeling bubbling up inside me. My mom is now braiding my sister June's hair—she's five—and chatting on the phone with one of my tías.

Mom looks up when I walk in, putting the phone down for a sec. "It seems like you have a new friend."

"Oh, he's going to be my best friend," I say.

* * *

Noah
Age sixteen

"So, like, you're gay, right?"

I'm standing next to my locker, looking for an escape route, because I really don't want to be having this conversation.

But I think I'm stuck.

"Um," I say, not sure how to answer. I mean, yes, I'm gay, but it's not something I talk about. And Kane doesn't have a filter about anything. I'd never tell him a secret, or it'd be all over campus in a matter of hours. At least no one seems to be paying attention to us right now.

Kane pats my shoulder as I zip up my backpack. "That's okay, you don't have to come out before you're ready. I just wanted you to know you're not alone."

"Um. Okay. Thanks." I nod a few times, unsure what else to say. Why is he talking to me? Everyone knows Kane's gay. "That's, um. Nice. Good for you."

His eyes widen suddenly. "Oh, I get it."

"You get what?"

"I was going to ask you out, but now I understand. You're dating August Ramirez!"

"Oh my god, be quiet," I hiss, making a "tamp it down" motion with my hands. "And no, definitely *not*. We're just friends. There's no way ... I don't like him like that."

"Sheesh," Kane says, blinking. "You're ... adamant."

I groan and slide my hands down my face. This isn't the first time someone's asked me about August. "It makes me annoyed, that's all. I don't understand why two people can't just be friends."

"Well, sure they can, sweetie pie."

"Okay. That's what we are. August is my best friend, but I'm not attracted to him like that. We're ... not like that at all." I'm lying through my teeth, but I couldn't handle it if I lost August.

I never knew my father. My mom has basically abandoned me in favor of dating one horrible man after another. The current one is a homophobic jerk who doesn't want to even know I exist. My grandma died last year from a stroke. All I have left is my grandfather, and he's getting older and starting to not remember things as well.

If I didn't have August, I'd have no one.

August doesn't want to date anyone seriously until he's at least thirty. He's told me so, many times. He's got big plans—like he wants to go to law school. I should go with him, he says. But even after law school, he says he doesn't want to get married, ever.

Besides, he doesn't think of me *like that.* He and I kissed once, last year, because neither of us had been kissed and we dared each other to do it. We've jerked off together a few times. When we tried to do more, though, it was very, very bad. I don't want to think about it. Suffice it to say, sex with August did *not* work.

But he and I *do* work as best friends. We talk about everything —almost. He goads me into playing sports, and I usually go along with it, because we always have fun together. We watch movies. We hang out.

A mainstay of our relationship—besides sports, movies, and hanging out—is pranking each other. Living next door to each other has its advantages for access to sneak around and mess with each other. For example, last month he put a life-size cardboard cutout of Chewbacca in my shower, which startled the crap out of me.

I got him back by secretly adding M&M's and Reese's Pieces to his jumbo bag of Skittles.

It's one way of having him pay attention to me.

But dating? Never. August invited Anita Sandoval to prom. I'll stay home with my grandpa.

I glance around, hoping no one's overheard my conversation with Kane. I have to be firm. He can't go thinking that I like August, or he'll tell August.

"August and I are best friends and nothing more," I continue, and slam my locker shut. "And that's the way it's always going to be."

CHAPTER 1

Noah

I n the darkened conference room, my phone lights up next to my laptop on the table, and it vibrates loudly, making my pulse race and my jaw clench. Out of the corner of my eye, I can see the bright, animated movement of a GIF.

Dang it. No. Not now. Of all the times …

I lunge forward and fumble to flip the device over. I had it out to use as a Wi-Fi hot spot, but I was so focused on my presentation that I forgot to protect myself.

Did they see?

Even through my panic, part of me wants to burst out laughing—because *jeez*, he got me. Except … I can't react. All I can do is continue as if nothing's wrong.

I glance around and let out a breath. I don't think they saw. At least I *hope* they didn't.

It's Friday afternoon, and I'm standing in an architecturally stunning office building in Venice—California, not Italy—surrounded by a dozen sharply dressed representatives of a potentially lucrative client: a major new LGBTQIA+ lobbying group. Shades cover the large windows, and the lights are off while a projector shows my PowerPoint presentation on a screen up front.

Pale orchids curve elegantly from their perches on sleek white tables.

What's waiting for me on my phone is as out of place as a stale Twinkie in a French restaurant.

Somehow, I manage to keep a straight face and continue with my pitch. I press my lips together, square my shoulders, and use the remote to click to my next slide. Fittingly, it's a photo of August and me from a few years ago, smiling in our suits as we cut the ribbon to our current offices. Well, he's cutting the ribbon. I'm fixing his tie. As usual.

"To bring this presentation to a close, I'd like to tell a little personal story, if I may," I say, smiling warmly. At least I hope it's warm and not a tension-induced grimace. "I founded the Weston & Ramirez law firm eight years ago with my best friend, August Ramirez, after we graduated from UCLA. We wanted to focus on LGBTQIA+ rights because we both had it pretty easy, all things considered. My grandfather raised me, and he's always been accepting. His only comment when I came out to him was, 'Dontcha put your pants on one leg at a time?' When I nodded, he said, 'So do I.' Of course, since he also says that about politicians he doesn't like, I'm not entirely sure it was a compliment." I get some polite laughter. "But seriously, my grandfather's great. August has a similar story. To his family, he's just another gay uncle. Or, rather, bisexual uncle. We're lucky." Or lucky enough, in my case. "Other people are not. We wanted to give them a voice."

I glance around the room, and I still have their attention. Maybe I can finish my spiel without any more disturbances. I switch to a slide illustrating some of our success stories and keep talking. "Among our recent accomplishments was having a part in drafting statutes for various states allowing both partners in a same-sex couple to be named on their children's birth certificates."

As I click to my last slide, I feel an anticipatory fluttering in my belly. Two reasons for that: I might have won a new client. More importantly, I think I made it through this meeting without my cell phone tanking my career.

I gesture at the screen, hoping my arm is steady as I use the laser on the remote to circle my email address and phone number next to our logo. "I'll be happy to answer any questions you have today, but if something comes up later, please contact me here for more information. We'd love to help you reach your goals. Thank you." The lights go back on, and someone flicks another switch to raise the window shades. I give the audience my most winsome smile, straightening my lucky tie.

The CEO, Steven with a *v*, smiles at me. "Thank you, Noah. I'll be the first to say your presentation is pretty compelling. We'd like to hire a firm led by people who have a stake in the results of our work."

I let out a small sigh of relief. While nothing's certain until they sign the engagement letter and send in the retainer, I think I reeled them in. This kind of success always gives me a rush.

But before I can reply, my phone buzzes again, the rattling noise and the light shining down on the glass table making everyone in the room focus on it. My stomach sinks to the below-ground parking garage.

On some level, I have to admit that the situation is hilarious. I know more or less what's waiting for me. Now, though, is most definitely *not* the time ... which is *precisely* why these particular texts were sent. August figures I can handle anything. Plus, we're in a comfortable enough position that if I don't nab this client, we'll be fine. I just wouldn't want the reason why I failed getting out. It wouldn't do my public image any favors, to say the least.

I nod, my cheeks burning. "We very much do have a stake in it. Everyone who works at Weston & Ramirez is either queer or an ally. While we also do general litigation and transactional work, the heart of the law firm has been its focus on advocacy."

"Having Sam Stone on your team is an advantage," says Stephen with a *ph*, the policy director.

I'm about to expound on how Sam's connections are unique and useful—he's the grandson of California's governor—when another buzz interrupts us.

Oh, for Pete's sake.

"Do you need to get that?" Steven with a *v* asks, gesturing like he's going to pick up my phone to hand it to me.

My heart beats so fast I think I'm going to pass out, and I start planning my own funeral. "Oh, no. It'll wait." I hastily snatch the phone and shove it into my interior jacket pocket.

I get a satisfied smile from the CEO. Like he's glad I'm ignoring my other responsibilities to focus on them.

If he only knew ...

"Because of Sam, we have a direct line to influence policy, and his grandfather can open doors." I look each one of them in the eye. "While August and I have a happy ending to our story—" I cough. "I mean, to our *coming out* stories, so many people don't, including members of our own staff. We wanted to create a power-house law firm where we could focus on the simple philosophy that love is love."

The attendees glance at each other. Stephen with a *ph* smiles and says, "We'll have to discuss this internally, but it's likely we'll recommend hiring your firm to our board of directors. Why don't you send us an engagement letter?"

Yes. "I'll do it right away. You'll get it no later than Monday afternoon."

Grinning, I shake his hand, then the hands of everyone else in attendance. Once the meeting is concluded, I pack up my laptop and projector and hightail it out as fast as I politely can. Not until I get safely out to the car do I check my phone.

And oh, goodness gravy yes, I am *so* glad I didn't do that during the meeting, because displayed on my screen are a series of GIFs of a guy sitting in a chair with another man on his lap, both facing the camera. The man on top is being lifted and fucked.

I tilt my head. The porn stars are both hot as heck, with six-pack abs, a smattering of tattoos, and enthralled expressions. The one getting it has a decent-sized schlong and a sexy hip tattoo, and he's getting plowed by a beast with tattoos down his arms and a monster cock. I laugh out loud, then snort, then cover my mouth with my hand, even though there's no chance of anyone seeing me right now.

I text my best friend, not needing to look this one up. Because reasons.

NOAH

What is elevated doggy style?

AUGUST

Correct

How did your presentation go

I can almost hear his snickering.

Some people prank each other by replacing toothpaste with that tomato paste that comes in tubes. *Amateurs.*

Although we've pranked each other since we were teens, since college, August and I have played this game called Poorly Timed Porn GIF Jeopardy, or PG for short—although the name is misleading, since there's nothing PG about it.

It started when he accidentally sent me a porn GIF while I was at dinner with my grandfather. He'd meant to send me a different picture. I was so mortified I dropped my phone on the floor, and then I couldn't retrieve it fast enough, and eventually, I was reduced to a stammering mess. To this day, I don't know if my grandfather figured out what was wrong with me.

August, who doesn't mind me knowing his porn preferences ... or anything else about him ... fell off his chair laughing when he found out. That was the first and only time he pranked me by accident.

I got revenge the next time we were at one of his family dinners. Turnabout's fair play. I made sure he got a particularly spicy clip while he was talking with his abuelita and his trio of nosy aunts. That shut him up.

Since then, it's morphed into a decade-plus-long contest where we send each other explicit GIFs at the worst possible time, and the recipient has to immediately identify the position. I've gotten quite an education over the years. Bully. Reverse crab. Wheelbarrow. I have a site with a naughty GIF dictionary of sorts to work off of, but I don't know where he gets his material.

We're not allowed to change the setting on our phone that shows a preview of the texts, so if anyone glances at our screen, they'd get a thumbnail of hard-core gay sex. Which is why my phone is normally in my pocket, or at the very least, facedown.

The irony—hypocrisy?—is strong, since we're lawyers and train people on how to not sexually harass others. Obviously, between the two of us, this is totally consensual. We just have to keep it hidden from anyone who might not want to see it—which makes the whole thing somewhat ill-advised. More than somewhat. The truth is, it's a spectacularly bad idea, but I do things with August I can't explain. Like play this game. We'll go months without sending anything, and then there are days like today ...

After smiling at his text, my fingers dance across the screen.

NOAH

It was one of my better efforts.

Until some jackhole sent me porn and tried to wreck my concentration.

Good thing dog and pony shows are my superpower.

AUGUST

[GIF of guy laughing]

Okay, real talk ... I'm proud of you, man. You do shit I can't. You're badass at presenting and drumming up business. You always look so poised and like everything is under control

I feel all warm inside, because August's praise does things to me.

> AUGUST
>
> Guess that's why I can't help messing with you.
>
> But I'm glad you're my partner

A pang hits me because he means law partner, not partner in life.

> AUGUST
>
> I hope you'll always be
>
> Hiking tomorrow? Meet you at the trailhead at 8?

> NOAH
>
> Yeah, sure see you then

He's always trying to get me to do outdoor things with him, especially extreme sports. Hiking is a tame suggestion. He must be wanting to enroll us in some endurance race or mud run.

But I'd take skydiving with August, blindfolded, while over jellyfish-infested waters before risking our friendship by telling him how I really feel about him. I'd rather have him in my life as a friend than not at all.

I already drove my mom away by being myself. I can't lose my other half.

I look again at the hot GIF, wishing it was an offer, not a tease. Then I put my phone down, scrub my hands over my face, and turn on my car. I decide to head home to Santa Monica, passing a cannabis dispensary and Erewhon, the snooty health food store, because yes, we live in Southern California. Under normal circumstances, I'd beeline back to our offices in Century City and open up the new file for the client I just landed, then celebrate with a glass of wine. Our firm has a happy hour every Friday in the break room, and it's rare for me to miss it.

But I don't feel like going today. It's not because I'm unhappy. Far from it. I'm very happy we have more business, and August made me laugh, as always. It's just ... *complicated*.

He's been my best friend since we were nine—twenty-five years now. We share everything. I know what he ate for breakfast today (egg whites with salsa in a corn tortilla) and how he got the scar on his wrist (bike accident when he was eighteen). He knows similar things about me. He's seen me laugh and yell and cry. He's gotten into fights to protect me. He's made me forget bad times and helped me create new, good ones.

You'd think, with us being best friends who work together, play together, live next to each other, and send each other porn as a joke, that there'd be no secrets between us. You'd be wrong, though.

August doesn't know I'm desperately in love with him.

CHAPTER 2

August

My thighs are burning as I hike the steep canyon incline in front of Noah, headed to the top of some peak in the Santa Monica Mountains. It's Saturday morning, and the air is scented with dust and sage, a dry Southern California potpourri that comes from silvery plants that barely need any water.

"Missed you at happy hour yesterday," I say.

Noah clears his throat. "Yeah, I know. I couldn't make it. I had that presentation in Venice, and by the time I was done, I figured you guys would be pretty much closed up."

"Oh? You had something important going on?" I aim for an innocent tone. "Did I know about that?"

"You're such a brat. You know you won," he admits. We pause at a switchback to catch our breath. Panting, he wipes a bead of sweat from his brow with the sleeve of his hoodie. The day is starting to get warm, but he hasn't taken his outer layer off yet. "Stunningly awkward timing. Where'd you find those GIFs?"

"I have my sources." I smirk and keep moving.

I created the GIFs myself from a particularly hot video I watched the other day, but I'm not going to share that with Noah.

He thinks I just look up gay porn positions on Urban Dictionary and then search Google for ready-made GIFs.

Adorable, naive man.

Nope, my research is more in-depth. It's no hardship to study videos looking for the perfect sex positions to send him at the worst possible times. Teasing him, daring him, pushing him to do things he wouldn't normally do is my specialty—my life's work, apart from the law stuff. And if I can make him blush, all the better.

There's a deeper meaning to our game, though. I know I'm being philosophical about a goofy game, but stay with me.

With everyone else, Noah is the height of respectability. The man wears a suit to work even if he's not seeing clients, gets his hair cut every ten days, and has old-fashioned manners. He always makes sure my buttons are done up correctly, and he gets his shoes polished whenever he sees a shoeshine stand.

And none of that is superficial. He puts his all into our firm. He's thoughtful, sensible, and professional. He's genuinely kind and caring.

In short, Noah's a good person.

Still, everyone needs a break. Being able to see who he really is —faults and all—is a privilege I don't take for granted. Even if that somehow translates into us sending each other porn at the worst possible moment and occasionally smoking dope.

We all have our thing.

As far as I know, I'm the only one who talks about dirty shit with Noah, gets him to swear, and spends this much time with him. Pretty sure I'm the only one he ever gets mad at—which I love, weird as it sounds, since he's all wound up, and his attempts to exact revenge for my pranks are the only way he lets loose. I'd rather poke at him and have him release his stress at me than have him internalize everything.

With me, Noah can be himself—all of himself, not just the parts he wants the public to see. So I'm not going to let up on the teasing anytime soon. If I can make him laugh, or be embarrassed, or both, I'm gonna do it.

"Fine," he grumbles. "Don't share your secret sauce."

"We all have to have some secrets, Dos." I call him Dos, as in Spanish for two. Because of Noah's ark. "Go find your own material. I know you beat off to it anyway."

Noah scowls at me. "You're such an asshole."

I got him to curse—or at least use vulgarity. Success!

Taking the opportunity for another brief stop, I turn around and put both hands on his shoulders. "Tell me your phone was face up when it happened."

Our eyes lock for a moment. Then he tears his gaze away and stares at the cloudless sky. "Ugh. Yes. I'm so disappointed in myself, because I'm not new at this. But no one saw."

"Dammit. I wish you'd've been caught," I cackle.

"Argh," he groans. "Why are you my best friend?"

I grin and give him a gentle shove. "Because you love me."

He mutters something and passes me. I adjust the straps on my day pack and then follow him up the path.

Noah's a little shorter than me and much leaner, with wavy light hair and blue eyes. His childhood freckles have mostly faded, although you can still see some on the bridge of his nose. He has a dimple in each cheek, and they flash when he's really amused. It's a good day when I get to see those dimples.

We hike along a stand of bright yellow Scotch broom. As we go, Noah plucks some blossoms and starts arranging them like he's making a bouquet.

When we get to a shady spot under an oak, I stop, chest heaving, and point at him. "You gonna take me to prom?"

"Fuck off." That's two! It's a great day for Noah swearing. He swats my hand away and takes a drink from his water bottle. But I don't miss the edges of his mouth quirking up.

I spot the summit ahead. "Race you to the top! We're almost there." I kick it up a gear.

"That's what you always say," he grumbles, taking off behind me.

"We should try this trail on mountain bikes next time," I call over my shoulder.

"Nah."

"Please," I beg. "It'll be fun. I dare you."

"I dunno. When I think about bikes, all I do is see myself crashing like last time."

We were out biking a few months ago—on a dedicated bike path, no less—when a pedestrian popped up in front of him. He swerved and ran into a barrier, and he hasn't stepped on a bike since. "Life's too short not to take risks."

"I'd argue that's a reason to be more careful," Noah insists.

I hold a branch out of the way so it doesn't thwap him in the face. "Take a risk, Dos. If you actually do shit, you don't have time to worry about it. Be in the moment. I dare you."

"I take plenty of risks." Noah crosses his arms over his chest as we continue up the hill.

"Not this kind."

"I'm traumatized by childhood horror stories about kids who hit a pebble wrong and killed themselves."

"Did that keep you off a bike at the time?" I ask.

"Well, no."

"Were the kids in these stories wearing a helmet?"

"I don't think so."

"So wear the damn helmet. You can't focus on what's gonna go wrong. Focus on how badass it is to go balls out down a hill. If you go rafting, you have to watch the water, not the rocks. Same thing."

He sighs, but I know he'll be back on a bike soon enough.

When we get to the top, I take in the 360-degree panorama, then walk over to the view of the Pacific Ocean to our west. There are huge new houses with swimming pools to the south, open space to the east and north.

Bending at the hips, I put my hands on my knees to catch my breath. Noah coughs behind me.

"You okay?" I ask, looking over my shoulder.

"Yeah," he says. "That was steeper than I remember."

Eventually, my heart rate evens out, and I go over to peer down a rocky ledge. Noah stands so we're shoulder to shoulder, and he offers me a sip from his water bottle before taking a drink himself.

There are a few people up here already, but given that we're still in Los Angeles County, that's the equivalent of being alone. I sit down on an outcropping that overlooks some people's backyards. No one's visible right now, so I don't totally feel like a peeping tom.

Noah joins me on the rock, his shoulder again brushing mine. Even though he's been hiking, he still smells good. Like his body wash, or whatever it is he uses in the shower.

"You know I'm gonna get you back," he mutters.

"Are you still going on about my texts?"

"Yes." He turns to me, shading his eyes from the sun. "They were so epically badly timed. *Sheesh*, man."

"Yeah," I say, giving him a smile. His face falls, and I reach out and grab his bicep. "Hey. What's wrong?"

Noah swallows a sip of water and looks down at his feet. "Do you think we're being too juvenile? Should we quit playing PG?"

"Do you want to?" I ask immediately. "I will, of course. I didn't know you didn't like it." I kick my dangling feet out. "I thought it was funny."

He turns and smiles wickedly. God, I love that smile. When he turns it on me, it's like the sun coming out on a cloudy day. "It *is* funny. When it's only the two of us, I think it's hilarious. But then I wonder how other people might take it. If some of our employees saw our texts?" He lets out a breath. "Man. They'd think we were sexting."

"I know, right?"

"And we could get in deep doo-doo. I mean, that kind of thing creates a hostile work environment."

"I don't think most of our staff would care."

Noah sighs loudly. "Probably not, but ... you never know. I'd never want to make someone feel uncomfortable."

I rub my nose. "So are we stopping?"

We look at each other and grin. "Nah," we say at the same time.

"We'll just be careful not to let anyone see who shouldn't," he says.

"That's always been the deal," I say, pushing him with my shoulder. "It's one of our things. Like training together." Then I get an idea. "You know what? We should do the Century Super Sprint Triathlon."

"Oh my god, why?"

"Because it's there. You know you want to." I grin. "I dare you."

Noah mutters something, but I take it as assent. He fusses with the yellow flowers he's picked, then hands me one.

"So we *are* going to prom," I joke.

"Give me that back," he says, and reaches for the bloom.

I hold it out of reach, laughing.

He shoves me, and I end up sprawled on my back in the dirt, laughing, holding the flower away from him. As he's trying to get at it, he hauls a leg over my waist, and while it's not the first time we've wrestled—we used to do it a lot as kids—it's the first time in a while.

We pause for a moment, panting, and then kind of take in how we ended up. He's straddling me, reaching for the flower, and I'm under him, looking up. His hair is mussed from the hike, and he's glowing from the exercise.

"Fuck you," he mutters—he's on a swearing roll, yes! He shoves my pecs and climbs off. As he walks a few feet away, I notice he's adjusting his shorts.

Shit. Did that just make him hard? I mean, he kind of made me chub up. What else is going to happen when someone's ass is on my groin?

I stand up and join him. I slap an arm across his shoulders, and together we look out at the view. "Shall we get going?"

"Yeah," he says, and swallows thickly.

I'm missing something.

* * *

Saturday evening I knock on Noah's door, then open it with my key. I'm not sure why I bother knocking, except I wouldn't want to catch him, like, with his pants down.

Not that Noah's ugly or anything. Far from it. He's a good-looking guy. Anyone could see that. I've thought for a while that he has some of the nicest eyes I've ever seen. They're gray-blue, like a washed-out sky, and they make me think of no one but him.

But he's never been interested in me. He made that clear so many years ago that it's not something I think about. Much.

"Hey," he says, looking up from his phone, those eyes bright on me. He's wearing joggers and a white T-shirt. "Pad thai or panang curry?"

My two favorites.

"Pad thai," I say, going over to his stainless steel fridge and putting in a six-pack, though I pull two out before I close the door.

"And fresh rolls?"

"You know it."

To other people, the comfort level I have with Noah probably wouldn't seem normal. I don't need to tell him I'm coming over—only if I'm not. I don't even need to tell him my order at a restaurant. I love that he knows me so well.

I grin and open our beers. Then I put the opener all the way away because Noah likes things just so. I even put the caps in the right place, i.e., the trash.

We live in the same condo complex in Santa Monica, a few doors down from each other. I spend as much time at his place as I do at mine, so we should've just bought one bigger one. But he wanted to do it this way. Our condos are a modern design with some peekaboo views of the ocean—his view is better, though. I love it here.

I Venmo him half the cost for the food and plop down in the middle of the couch. That leaves him no choice but to sit kind of close, but we're always like this.

I have this theory that Noah was touch starved as a kid. When his mom dumped him with his grandparents, he needed hugs, and I supplied them. Nothing's changed after all these years. I'm still touchy-feely, so we usually end up with him lying on top of me. Everyone needs affection.

"Are we still on season one of *The Mandalorian*?" I ask, as I pick up the remote.

"Yup." Noah leans so his head is on my chest, and my arm stretches along the back of the couch.

Noah's not into any particular actor or director. No. He likes a particular *cinematographer*, so we've been making our way through Greig Fraser's entire catalog. I start the show, and we settle in, with him kind of on top of me.

The food comes partway through our second episode, and we end up eating on the couch. When the credits roll, I turn to him. "You tired or want to watch a movie?"

"I could go for a movie after we clean up this stuff." He gestures to our plates. "But I'm feeling lazy."

"I'll take care of it. Want a hit?"

He grins. "Sure."

I'm surprised every time my goody-two-shoes best friend agrees to get high with me, but he says it's legal, and he's an adult, and he only does it when he's not going to drive anywhere.

After I tidy our meal detritus and turn down the lights, I pull the vape pen out of my pocket and hand it to him.

Noah reads the side and smirks. "'GS Cookies.' Who do they think they're kidding?" He sucks on the vape, then passes it to me. I take a hit and lie back on the couch.

"*The Batman*?" I ask, returning the pen and clicking the remote.

"Sure."

I start the movie. "C'mere."

Noah sits in front of me, his back to my chest, and leans on me. I always breathe easier when we're like this.

"You feel like home," I say. "I'm not sure why we don't live together."

"You'd get sick of me." He inhales from the pen again.

"Nah." I run my fingers through his hair, enjoying how soft it is. "Your hair is almost golden," I say, and take another toke. I'm sleepy and warm. I have my best friend cuddling with me. In some ways, we're like that Danish term "hygge," meaning cozy comfort. Noah's hygge to me. "You're, like, a golden boy."

"Ha." He accepts the vape pen from me and takes another hit. I like watching him. I like the way his chest fills up and then he lets the vapor out. "You could be Batman, though."

"I'm hot enough to be a badass superhero," I agree.

"Yeah." Noah's voice sounds dreamy.

I inhale from the vape again and then reach over and drop it on the table.

Noah burrows more into me. "Wait, you can't be Batman."

"Why not?" I brush his hair with my hand.

"You're not emo enough."

I laugh. "Yeah, you're not emo either."

"Except about my parents." He adjusts the pillows under us. "Hey, I'm kinda like Batman with the shit with my parents."

"Nah, dude. Your mom's still around, and your gramps."

"Kinda." He goes quiet.

"Hey," I say. "We don't have to talk about family."

"Then we can talk about this fucking cinematography," he

murmurs. He must be buzzed, if he's swearing.

"Yeah. And Nirvana." But the volume's too low. My lips almost brush his ear as I reach for the remote. "Sorry," I say, tugging on the lobe. I turn the sound up. "Settle back down." I wrap my arms around him, and we watch the story unfold, comfortably baked. "How come you like this cinematographer so much?" I ask a little later.

"Because he's really in charge. Yeah, some say the director or the writers or the actors. But the whole look of the movie is the DP's job."

I smirk. "The DP?"

He shoves me. "Director of photography. Not, um. You know."

"Dual penetration."

"Is it dual or double?" he asks.

"Yeah, you're right. Double."

"Okay. And now I know what GIF I'm sending you next."

That makes me laugh. "Would you ever try it?" I say, yawning. "Photography?"

"Dual penetration. I mean double."

"Uh, no. I just want one guy at a time."

"What about with a dildo or something?"

He shrugs. "Maybe."

"But that doesn't answer my original question. You distracted me. I think you like the way this photographer is on the outside looking in. Like that opening shot, looking through the windows. It's like he's spying." I yawn again, feeling happy and relaxed. "He's spying on a family. Maybe you want that."

"Hmm. Maybe. Or maybe I like to watch more than participate. Less risk."

"More fun to do shit, though," I say.

Now he's yawning, too, and eventually, we drift off to sleep, the show music droning on.

I feel like I'm right where I belong.

CHAPTER 3

Noah

After working hard all week, on Fridays, everyone at our office is ready to loosen up. August and I have held happy hours ever since we started W&R, to encourage collegiality. After all, part of being in a smaller law firm is that people get to know each other. More than that, though, August likes to throw parties ... and I like to make him happy.

This Friday, happy hour has moved from our break room to One, our go-to gay club. One is huge, with multiple levels, and while the dance floor and main bar are loud, there are quieter nooks in other areas. We tend to congregate in one of them so we can talk, and we often get the same server. Alice (yes, women can work at gay clubs) has a big personality and an incredible memory for faces, names, and orders.

She's shot the shit with us enough to know our dating histories, family dramas, and work successes and failures. I'm pretty sure all of us consider her a friend and even a confidant. Bartenders keep a lot of secrets, and so does Alice.

"So, you and Alden?" Alice asks Danny, one of our partners. August and I hired Danny pretty quickly after we opened the firm, because we recognized that he was a go-getter like us. He's also become a good friend.

Danny has his arm slung around Alden, our shy bookkeeper. Danny's tall and handsome, with an easy confidence and a great look. Until recently, he was infamous for being the king of One— and one-night stands—but Alden seems to have hooked him. Danny kisses Alden's cheek. "Aren't I lucky?"

Alden blushes.

"I don't know what you did to tame that beast," Alice tells Alden, "but I think it's awesome."

"I do, too," Danny says, beaming.

Alice whips around to August. "And you? When are you going to get tamed?"

"Um, never. God," he says, and my heart sinks. I knew August was against marriage, but every time he says it, it hurts a little more. "I get enough of this from my family. I have to hear it from you, too?"

And this is why I never get my hopes up.

"Are you going to settle down with someone?" I ask Alice.

She sticks her hands in her pockets and rocks back on her heels. "No. So I want to live vicariously through all of you." She grins. "What can I say? I just want people to be happy. And if people can be happy when they're with someone else, then I get happy and the whole world lives in love."

"You sound like a Julian Hill song," August mutters.

"Hey," Sam says, shoving August's shoulder.

"I love his songs," August clarifies. "All I mean is that he's very sincere and earnest."

"Well, yes, he is." Sam gets a dopey grin on his face. The pop megastar is his boyfriend.

"And see," Alice says, gesturing at Sam. "Another happy couple."

"But why do we have to couple off?" August asks. "I've got my best friend. If I need something else, that's what hookup apps are for." He wraps an arm around me, and I rest my head on his shoulder. Then he rubs the top of my head, and I laugh and shove him.

Alice studies him for a very long moment. "I don't think I've ever seen you on a date."

"That's because I'm usually hanging with this guy," August says.

"You're best friends?" Alice asks.

"Yes," I say.

"And you hang out together all the time?"

August holds our hands out in an "exhibit A" gesture.

"Do you live together?"

"Close," Shelby tells her. He's our receptionist and also the eyes and ears of our firm. I'd be surprised if he doesn't know absolutely everything that goes on. "They're neighbors."

"Where is this going?" August asks.

"I dunno," Alice says slowly. "You two are very interesting. I wonder if being friends is enough."

August laughs and shoos her off. "Whatever. Go harass someone else."

"I'll bring your drinks," she says, but she doesn't leave.

"I agree with Alice," Danny says. "I don't get it. You guys are so close. You're best friends since forever. You practically live with each other. You co-own the firm. How come you guys aren't together?"

August answers for us. "We tried it once. Didn't work."

I smirk, although the reminder of our awkward attempts at sex when we were teens is embarrassing and painful. "Nope. Not for us."

"We were each other's first kiss, though," August says. "We dared each other to do it. And we tried more, but as Noah says, *nope.*"

I remember that fumbling kiss—how much my heart pounded, how hard my cock was. We wanted to get our first kiss over with, so why not let it be with each other? But then his little sister June walked in, and it was over. A week later, we tried more, and that didn't work at all.

#scarredforlife

"What happened?" Danny asks.

"Ugh," I say. "Let's leave it that we were adolescent boys and messing around, and it did not go well. Also ..." I look around. "Should we really be talking about sex at a work function?"

"It's not like that's ever stopped us before," Shelby says.

"Yeah, but," I insist, feeling slightly guilty. We should be better than that. We're supposed to set an example.

"Noah's right," August says.

"Now I feel like I'm disappointing you," I say, looking around at everyone's faces. I open my mouth, and everyone leans in to listen. "It really isn't that big a deal. Just ... use your imagination and think of the worst things two gay teens—"

"Bi," August corrects.

"One bi and one gay fifteen-year-old could come up with, and you'd be on the right track. Needless to say, we didn't have any chemistry—"

"Or lube," August adds. "Or prep—"

"And we couldn't figure out how things worked. It hurt and was bad and awkward. We stayed friends instead."

August slides an arm around my shoulder and drags me close. "The best of friends." He smells too tempting as he kisses the side of my head.

I clink my empty bottle to his nearly full one.

Alice narrows her eyes. "If you say so."

"Come dance," Danny says to us, when Alden tugs him up.

"Nah, I don't feel like it," August says, holding up his beer.

Danny turns to me. "Coming?"

I shrug. "Sure."

I walk with Alden and Danny to the dance floor. Almost immediately, they're wrapped up in each other like they're one body, which is to be expected since they're squarely in the honeymoon phase of their relationship. A big, bear-type dude comes up to me, but since he's not August, I'm not interested. I scoot in a different direction. Soon I'm in the middle of a few guys who are writhing, and I get lost in the music.

One guy starts grinding up on me, and I let him, even though he's rather handsy. It's not like I'm going to get any action from the one I actually want, after all. I'm not going to go home with this guy or anything, but I'm good with dancing.

When he moves in for a kiss, though, there's a tap on my shoulder. I turn around, and August is standing there, dark eyes hard. He lifts his chin to the other guy. "Hey," he says with a fake smile. "Thanks for keeping him company." He wraps his arms around my waist and tugs me to him.

And then I'm dancing with August, which is wonderful and horrible at the same time. He's a better dancer than I am, and when he holds me close, I feel everything: his strong back, his defined arms, how he moves. His dark hair gleams in the club lighting, and he looks delectable in his slacks and slim-fit dress shirt. He's let his usual fade haircut grow out a bit, and his curls are floppy.

He's such a beast of a man. He's been working out frequently, and he's gotten more buff, to the point where it's all I can do to not lick him. August isn't traditionally handsome—at least, I don't think so. He's not leading man pretty, like those models with too-big eyes and lips. He's all sharp angles and harsh edges, but there's something so eminently *masculine* about his looks that I can't keep my eyes off him. It's like someone crowdsourced a man—perfect and imperfect at the same time. Hot as heck, as far as I'm concerned.

We dance for a few songs, and then he says in my ear, "Had enough? Want to go home?"

I nod, and we exit the dance floor and say our goodbyes.

We walk to my car, the cool air nipping at us, a stark contrast to the club's hot, sweaty interior. "So, that guy dancing with you," August says as we pass a group of people smoking.

"Which guy?" I ask, even though I know who he's talking about. I love it when August is possessive of me, even though it doesn't mean what I wish it meant.

"The guy. You know. With the hair."

I laugh. "That doesn't narrow it down much."

August groans. "You know what I mean. Was he your type?"

"Nah," I say fast. *Because my only type is you.* "He was just there."

"Hmm." August falls silent. Then he asks, "What was up with Alice? Did it seem like she was being particularly nosy?"

"She seemed to think that you and I should be boyfriends."

He chuckles. "Can you imagine?"

Yes. Heck, yes. "No." My laugh is a little off, but maybe August won't notice.

"Me either." He clears his throat and then stares off into the distance.

Was August thinking about what it would be like if we were actually boyfriends?

Not that that's something I'd want. Not at all. Because denial is a fun and safe place. It's where I do my best work.

Although I'm not sure it really is denial if I *know* I'm denying my feelings. But I've read that the function of denial is protection from getting hurt, and I've been hurt enough by those I love. I don't need to sign up for more of it.

We pass another group of partiers before we get to my car.

"Do you want to go for a bike ride tomorrow?" August asks.

"Ugh, no." I scrub my face. "We should, shouldn't we?"

"If we want to be competitive in the triathlon, we really have to train."

"I haven't said yes."

"You haven't said no, either."

I sigh. "You're right. I'll do it. But I'm not sure I care about being competitive. I'll just want to be able to finish."

"Well, then that," he says with a smile. "I dare you."

I groan. "Okay, fine. But can we not go too early?"

"Yeah, it's late already. We don't have to kill ourselves. We just have to do it." He grins. "Or we could swim laps at the pool at our place."

I chuckle. August can't stick with one form of physical movement. One week we're doing sprint races, and the next he's decided that we're going to be playing in an inter-firm soccer league.

That's the way he is, though. With dates, too. I can't remember him ever seeing someone more than a few times. It's not quite one-night stands, but he doesn't have much patience with them.

I think our friendship is the only thing he's stuck with for his whole life, besides his family. I suppose that's how you can figure out what someone values.

I like that I'm something he values.

But it does seem like in matters of the heart, he's uncertain and goes out with whoever he can pick up on an app. I haven't met very many of them, and the ones I have seen make me want to throw things.

In fairness, my own relationships have been short-lived and shallow. I don't mean for them to be. It just happens ... because they're not him.

August's never liked any guy I've been seeing, either. He gets all growly, and even though it's annoying, I secretly like it. Or maybe not so secretly.

"Fine. We'll go swimming tomorrow," I agree, looking forward to the idea of August shirtless, in trunks. I drive us home and, as usual, he comes inside with me instead of going to his own condo. We fall asleep on my couch watching *Dune.*

In the morning, after swimming, we go to our separate homes to get ready for the day. August is faster than me, so when he's dressed, he comes back to my place, and I can hear him in my kitchen making breakfast while I'm still showering. As I exit the bathroom, I smell eggs and bacon.

I'm in my bedroom sliding on my T-shirt when my phone rings. August pops his head in to say, "Breakfast is warm in the oven," then sees my face and sits on the bed. "Who is that?"

Grimacing, I say, "Mom."

He nods, his face serious for once. He gestures to ask if I want him to leave, but I shake my head, and he stays put.

"Hi," I say, wary.

"Noah." My mom's voice is warm and makes my stomach ache because I always get my hopes up that ... what? She'll actually want to spend some time with me? "I wanted to let you know that I'm going to be out of town for a while. Raul is taking me to Italy!"

I pinch the bridge of my nose. "That's great, Mom." My voice doesn't sound sincere, even though I'm trying hard. "Have fun."

She prattles on. "I can't wait to show you all the pictures from where we're going. Venice, Florence, Naples. All over!" My mom goes through her Italian itinerary in great detail. She lowers her voice. "I really think he's the one, honey."

Oh, god. No.

This is why she left me with my grandparents in the first place. She got caught up in her "one true love"—a jerk who didn't want kids around—so she left me. And then that man dumped her and she found another—who was homophobic, so I *really* wasn't wanted. And then she found another. And another. But she's always questing for the one. Even though she's never found him.

Guess why I'm so hesitant about relationships. I'm sure it has nothing to do with my mom's rotating selection of boyfriends.

August looks at me questioningly. I must be showing my distaste for her life choices and grumpiness that they've affected me so much.

"What does Lewis think of this?" I ask into the phone.

"He's available and is going to water the plants!"

That didn't answer my question. My mom's best friend, Lewis, has put up with her crud for so long. He adores her, but she'll never look at him twice.

Again, not like it's clear where my issues come from or anything.

Lewis is great, though. He's always helped me when I needed it, shown up to things like our office opening when she didn't, even helped me learn to ride a bike when I was a kid.

August is messing with his phone, and I know that look on his face. He wants to tell me to hang up. He wants to protect me from her. But he also knows that I'll always be polite to her and listen. She is my mom, after all.

When she's finally done, I flop on the bed next to him. He runs a hand through my hair. "Hey," he says. I don't reply, and after a second, he scoots closer and pulls me into his arms. "Hey," he repeats quietly. "Are you okay?"

Gah. If he only pranked me and never showed that he cared, he would've been out of my life years ago. August messes with me *because* he cares about me, and it's beautifully awful. His protective streak is one of my favorite things about him.

I don't say anything, because there's nothing to say. He's always been there when my narcissistic mom shows up, and he knows I need a minute.

Except he doesn't know that I feel like I'm Lewis—standing on the side, in love with my best friend who doesn't return the feelings.

"Want some coffee?" he asks after a moment.

"Yeah."

Neither of us make a move to go anywhere. Why would I want to? I have everything I need, being right here in his arms.

CHAPTER 4

August

On Thursday night, I tug on Noah's hand and whine, "Dos, save me" as we walk up to my abuelita's house and hear the noise spilling out into the night.

He gives me a wide grin, looking at the front door. "What am I supposed to save you from?"

"My tías."

He gives me an "Ah" in recognition. Because he's been around enough to know that my aunts are demons from a different dimension. Saucy demons in high heels and halter dresses that show off shapely shoulders and full, long, dark waves of hair. They're gorgeous. Even I can tell that.

But they're demons.

"What do you want me to do?" Noah asks, straightening the collar of my short-sleeved buttoned shirt. "Get something to vaporize them?"

"Good idea. That would help." I pull out my vape and take a hit, then hand it to him.

Noah stares at it. "That's not what I meant."

"We won't drive for a while," I assure him.

He nods and sucks on the pen, then gives it back to me.

"You're forgetting that I've known them for years. They won't be all that bad—"

"August and Noah," Flor singsongs as she flings open the door, "come talk to me and your tías."

"Dammit," I say under my breath.

I follow her into the living room, and Noah comes along without me needing to tug him. This is why—one of the reasons why—he's my best friend. It's like he's geared up for battle. Except the adversaries are wearing fuchsia lipstick and have big fake flowers pinned to the side of their hair. And I love them.

My grandma's definitely the matriarch of our family. My grandfather died young, so she had to raise six children by herself: my mother and my three aunts, plus two boys. One of my uncles lives in Vegas now, but everyone else is still here in LA.

My aunts are the kind of women who always wear their hair nicely done, full makeup, dresses, and high heels. And most of the time, they're sipping from something alcoholic, usually with a long stem. Today they hold margaritas in clear glasses with blue rims as they surround me in the living room.

"August! You decided to come. And you brought Noah with you. Good." Abuelita is tiny but fierce in her black dress.

"Hello. Thanks for having me over," he says, leaning forward and kissing her on the cheek. Then he kisses my mom, and then each of my aunts, Flor, Soledad, and Rosa, because he's genuinely a good person. He stands to the side and starts talking with my mom. My dad gives me a chin lift from across the room where he's listening to one of my cousins. At least he's out being social. That's good. The sliding glass doors are open, showing lots of other relatives outside.

"Hi, Tía Flor," I say, giving her a kiss. She pinches my cheek in return. I swivel my head. "And Tía Soledad. And Tía Rosa. You all look beautiful."

They preen. Then they turn their savage knives on me. "So,

August. Tell us how you are doing. Do you have a boyfriend? Or a girlfriend?" Tía Rosa says.

"Nope."

Rosa sips her drink. She points to my prom picture, which is on the crowded mantel along with school pictures of all my cousins. "Is that the last girl you took out?"

"What? No. I've dated women since then." If you call hookups dating.

Noah's engrossed in his own conversation and not saving me from this one, but I'm going to mess with him. When he sees me pull out my phone, he shakes his head subtly and rolls his eyes, very deliberately sticking his phone in the back pocket of his jeans.

"Chicken," I mouth.

"What are you saying, August?" my abuelita says, knocking me back to the present moment. "We have pollo asada."

"Thank you," I say, grinning. Noah goes back to his conversation with my mom. It warms my heart that he spends time with her, not only because it means a lot to my mom, who's had a rough time of it, but because it gives him some much-needed Mom time.

"August," Soledad says, keeping me from sending Noah any inappropriate GIFs. "Tell me who you are dating."

I choke out a laugh. "No one." I glance outside to where my siblings, uncles, cousins, and various other relatives are milling around. I want to escape to talk with them. I see Tío Raymond— our family's original gay uncle—laughing with my youngest sister, April, who's now twenty-six. May is now twenty-eight and married, as is June, who's thirty. Her kids are running around everyone's legs in the yard.

"That can't be true. Handsome man like yourself has plenty of dates," Rosa says. "You need to settle down."

"Why?" I ask, genuinely wanting to know.

"Because it is your destiny. You need to find yourself a nice person to make you happy."

"Maybe he doesn't need anyone because he has Noah," Flor chides.

I shake my head. "Noah's just a friend."

"Mm-hmm," Rosa says. "You're bound to find someone. You're handsome. You have money and a house."

"Is that all I have to offer? My looks and material possessions?"

Soledad raises a manicured finger and lifts up my chin, inspecting me. "No, you have more than that."

"We just want you to be happy," Flor says.

"Are you bothering August?" my mom asks, breaking away from her conversation with Noah.

"Oh, August isn't bothered. He's just telling us he's fine on his own." Rosa sniffs, obviously not believing me.

"Why do you want me to date?" I ask. "I don't need a romantic partner."

"Because you have Noah?" Flor asks, a sparkle in her eye that annoys me.

"For the last time," I say, not really exasperated but headed there. They're always like this, though. "Noah and I are best friends. Nothing more."

"Hmm," Flor says. "You two would be so good together."

Noah's eyes go wide. "Uh, um. We don't …"

She puts a hand on her hip. "Why not? You have that chemistry. You should be together."

"But I'm not in love with Noah," I say. "Sorry, dude, you know I love you as a friend."

"Yeah," he says, his voice a little off. "I know. And, um. Me, too. I mean, same."

"See?" I say triumphantly. "We're just friends."

That's all Noah's ever wanted, anyway.

"Whatever you say," Rosa says. "I predict you'll get married within the next two years."

I roll my eyes. "For heaven's sake. No." When I think about my future, the only person in it, really, is Noah. I mean, since we have the firm together and everything.

"Do you want to get married?" I ask him.

He sputters. "To you?"

"No, dude. To anyone."

Noah nods. "Yes. I want to belong to someone. Not in some weird sense, but"—he shrugs—"I'd like to have someone in my corner. I want to know that someone chooses me, you know? And I'd like the strength in being part of a couple."

His words make my stomach feel funny. I don't want some guy taking him away from me.

"Well, you'll always have me in your corner, and if you get married, I'm still living near you," I announce.

For some reason, all three of my aunts get huge grins on their faces.

"Fine, August. If I get married, you'll still be my best friend," Noah says.

I throw an arm around his shoulder and escort him away from my relatives, throwing back at them, "Time for a drink."

I need it after dealing with them.

* * *

On Tuesday morning, I open the Los Angeles County Superior Court doors and step inside. This is a big motion I'm defending against: if the other side wins, we've essentially lost the entire case. I'm prepared but still worried.

I check in with the judicial assistant, then take my seat to wait for the judge's entrance. I do a chin up-nod when opposing counsel walks in. Just because he's my adversary doesn't mean he's a bad dude.

He checks in and sits across the aisle from me. I'm about to lean over to ask him his client's settlement position when my cell phone makes a loud noise.

I freeze.

Shit, shit, shit.

First of all, I'm not supposed to have my cell phone on in the courtroom. At a minimum, it's supposed to be on silent, and the bailiff is giving me a hard look. Worse, I know that ringtone. If I pull my phone out, it's going to have a preview GIF of porn on the home screen.

Shit.

I fumble with the device while the bailiff says, "All rise." And while I'm cursing Noah's name, I'm also admiring his initiative. Somehow I get the thing turned off before it buzzes again. Smiling at my feet, I shake my head, then take a few calming breaths to find my center before I have to argue the motion.

God, I love Noah. I can't wait to see what he sent me. DP, if he knows what's good for him. If not, I'll find some and send it to him later.

But when I get to the office—after my successful hearing—he's busy working on some plan to hire more attorneys and too distracted for me to bring up PG.

Expanding our business always gives me the heebie-jeebies. "Do you really think we should be hiring?" I ask. "I'm worried about the financial outlay."

"Ah, but if they get even close to the minimum billable hour expectations," Noah says, "and ours are the most reasonable in the building, look at what we'd net." I look over his shoulder and then shrug.

Money decisions like this make me nervous, but I trust him.

"Sounds good," I say. And let him steer our business toward world domination. Or whatever it is he's doing.

* * *

On Friday night, we're back at One, music pumping, our friends ordering drinks and dancing. Noah sees Alice and groans. "Are we going to get harassed again?"

"What do you mean?" I laugh. "Is she going to ask us to go get dates or whatever?"

"Right."

"Probably." I grin, and Noah manages a smile in return. "By the way, I forgot to ask why you sent me a GIF of a dude bent over a desk and not a DP," I say into his ear.

Noah shrugs. "I couldn't find one." He reddens. "I found that one while I was looking, and I thought it was hot."

Shelby scoots in on my side of the booth and wiggles. "What's hot? I'm gonna find me some hot man tonight."

I laugh. "Go get 'em, tiger."

"I'm not a tiger, I'm a twink."

"You're the best twink ever."

"Right? I know." He's wearing a pink V-neck T-shirt that's sparkly and see-through and very tight. He must have gone home and changed—or brought a change of clothes with him to work. Sometimes we come here straight from the office, taking off ties and jackets. Other times we dress more club-like, but that's usually when we end up going later. Tonight, I'm in a slim-fit dress shirt and slacks, having come here directly from court. Noah's wearing pretty much the same thing, but we've unbuttoned the top buttons and rolled up our sleeves, so we don't look *so* corporate.

Shelby is definitely not in office attire. You can see his nipples through his shirt, and I'm sure any guy would want to tap his very perky ass.

Well, not *any* guy. I mean, I'm not interested. But I'm not interested in anyone, generally speaking. I hang with Noah, and that's good enough for me.

"What are you two doing these days?" Shelby asks.

"I talked Noah into training for the Century Triathlon," I say.

Shelby's eyes widen. "Wow. You're always doing that kind of

stuff." He yawns. "I'd much rather eat marshmallows on the couch."

"Me, too," Noah mutters, and I elbow him.

Danny and Alden join us from the dance floor, panting, and Alice walks up to us, chewing gum.

"Are you auditioning for the part of 1950s waitress?" I ask, after our friends place their drink orders.

She gives me a sarcastic laugh. "Ha ha, no. I just know I'm gonna kiss someone tonight, and I want to have fresh breath."

"Who are you kissing?" Noah asks.

"Wouldn't you like to know." She smirks. "It's not like you boys kiss anyone anyway." She turns to Danny and Alden. "I'm not talking about you two." Then she tells Shelby, "Not you, either. You'll get some, I'm sure." Shelby giggles. "I mean these jokers." She gestures at me and Noah. "You two are beyond help."

Noah reddens.

I cross my arms over my chest. "What's that supposed to mean?"

"You're missing out on who you should be kissing," Alice says.

"Okay, tell me: who am I supposed to be kissing?" I ask.

She gestures at Noah. "Him."

The gust of air that comes out of me is embarrassing, and I try to pass it off as a laugh.

Danny guffaws.

"Noah?" I ask. I grin at him. "Do you want me to kiss you?"

"What? I, um. No?" He gulps. "What's the right answer here?"

"I have no idea," I say dryly.

"How about this," Alice says, pointing between me and Noah. "I dare you to kiss each other."

"I can't believe she said that," Alden says.

"I know, right?" Danny says, kissing his boyfriend's nose.

"What? That's infantile," Noah says.

Alice grins. "There's nothing infantile about kissing. Quite the opposite, actually."

"This is a dare?" I ask. "Why?"

"I think you won't do it."

"What do you think?" I ask Noah. "Want to kiss?"

"Not if it will ruin our friendship," he says.

I scoff. "Kissing isn't going to ruin our friendship. We did it before, and here we are." Noah's expression goes weird, so I pause and study him. "Hey, I'm not going to take some crappy dare if it's going to make you uncomfortable. Your friendship means more to me than that."

He smiles but then rolls his eyes. "I know, but I also know you don't like backing down from a dare. You dole them out enough. It's fine. It's really fine. If you want to."

"Watch and learn," I say to Alice. Sam, Shelby, Alden, Danny, and our other coworkers watch us, rapt.

I can't really believe I'm doing this, but I am. So, here goes.

I lean in to kiss my best friend. His plump lips part on an exhale, and his eyes look wary. But there's some heat in them, too, and I'm thinking he might want this. I think *I* might want this.

It's just a kiss. No big deal. We can move on.

Our lips brush—it's a whisper of a kiss. Just touching. But then he goes in for more. Or maybe it's me, and then we're pressing our lips together with such force that it knocks the breath out of me. So I open my mouth, and he takes the invitation to invade it with his tongue.

And oh, mamma, he tastes really good. He smells good. He feels good.

I swirl my tongue into his mouth, and my hands are gripping his cheeks, holding him to me. His hands are clasped behind my neck, so we're both drawing each other in, like we're binding ourselves to each other.

He makes an impatient noise in the back of his throat, and I can't even. I hold him closer, and that causes even more reactions. My dick stiffens. The blood thunders in my ears and pounds in my veins. I lose track of time.

Noah's overwhelming, and he's making something feral rise up inside me and try to claw its way out. I want to claim him.

I don't know that I've ever had a better kiss.

I've certainly never had a more breathless kiss. I've never felt something like this.

I'm shaken to my very center, and I don't know if I'm going to be able to recover.

Because I don't know if I want to.

We break apart, and I'm panting. So is he.

"Wow," Alice whispers. "That was so hot I almost came."

Noah's cheeks pink, and we both turn to her.

I clear my throat and wipe my mouth with the back of my hand. "Okay now?"

"Yeah," Noah says, his voice raspy. "Okay?"

All our friends stare at us. "Happy?" I ask.

They all nod.

* * *

I walk into my condo that night feeling like the world has changed.

What the fuck happened? Kissing Noah was ... hot. Noah was ... hot.

I mean, objectively, Noah's always been hot. He's in great shape. He's a handsome guy. He has clear skin and bright eyes and soft hair. And his ass ...

Okay, it seems that I've paid more attention than I realized to how my best friend looks.

But I've never thought about what he tastes like. I wrote us off so long ago, and I haven't really thought about it since.

A couple times when we were in our teens, we decided to watch porn together. And we both got hard. And we jacked off in the same room.

I didn't really watch him, but I wonder if he watched me.

I kind of like the idea that he might have.

The time we tried to do more, we were so young and fumbling. No wonder we never tried again.

But tonight. Noah's lips on mine. His hot breath. The way his eyes looked up close—the lighting in the club made the blue look very dark, with bits of gold I'd never noticed before. The freckles that you can't see unless you're close enough to kiss him. The way he smells like Dior Homme.

He made me hard.

My best friend. My buddy. My pal. The guy I've known since we were kids. The one I've never had more than platonic feelings for.

The one I haven't *allowed* myself to have feelings for, because he's not into me.

Made me hard.

I had to get out of there. He probably thought I fled (thankfully we hadn't driven together) because I was offended—even though he knows I don't get offended easily. Or that something was wrong.

Something *was* wrong.

I … liked kissing Noah. I liked it a lot. It felt *right*. It felt like coming home.

And I'm not sure what to do with that information. Do I tell him? How will he react?

What if it was just a normal kiss to him, when to me it was … eye-opening to say the least. More like mind-blowing.

Where did Noah learn to kiss like that?

I'm pacing the living room, and I never pace. I'm known for being cool and collected.

Not now.

"Fuck!" I run my hands through my hair, tugging on the ends. "What the hell, Noah?"

The problem is … The problem is, I'm still horny, and if I do anything about it, I'm going to be beating off to images of my best friend—specifically, a mental reenactment of that kiss.

Fuck it.

I barely make it into my bedroom before I'm ripping my fly open, grabbing lube, and jerking myself as fast as I can. My cock is like a damned pole, and my hand is racing up and down it because I'm so damn desperate and pent up. Like I'm going to explode if I don't let all this sexual energy out.

Remembering Noah pressed against me. It felt so right. It felt so hot.

Like he was mine.

In no time at all, I'm coming all over my hand with a shout, a big fucking mess.

I slump against the dresser and take in my surroundings. I'm standing here with my pants shoved down to my thighs, my dick in my sticky hand.

The orgasm released my anxious energy, but I'm still troubled. Because I never navel-gaze like this. I'm not introspective. I just act. I ride my bike. I bungee jump. I go out for a run.

I don't contemplate changing my relationship with Noah.

Do I even want to?

I kick my pants the rest of the way off and shrug out of my shirt, wiping my hands on it. I get into the shower for a quick scrub, but when the hot water hits me I find I'm thinking about what it would be like if I had Noah in here with me.

I'm getting aroused again, but it's bad enough I've already beaten off to the memory of our kiss. I can't make it worse by fantasizing about doing very naughty things to him.

And they are *very* naughty things. I'm picturing his toned torso and defined shoulders, his curly hair and perfect ass and ... *fuck*.

I need to stop. I get out of the shower, still hard, and dry off.

My phone buzzes.

NOAH

Hey, you okay?

I'm sorry about the kiss, Mes.

He hasn't called me "Mes" in a while. It's been his nickname for me since we were kids: Spanish for month, because ... August.

NOAH

I know you can't back down from a dare.

But just ...

Don't worry about it, okay?

Not that you were worried.

Sorry, I'm overthinking

AUGUST

All good. Sorry was in the other room.

Specifically the shower, thinking about you, but we'll set that little detail to the side and let it sit there unacknowledged.

AUGUST

Hey, I can tell my best friend that he's a damned good kisser.

<heart emoji>

NOAH

Okay, good.

Good night

AUGUST

Night

I appreciate the fact that he's trying to soothe me and I'm trying to soothe him, but I'm not sure what's ruffling our feathers.

Except the fact that we kissed, and now everything has changed.

CHAPTER 5

Noah

Saturday morning, I pace around my home wringing my hands.

I may *unalive* Alice, as the TikTok kids say. What the *heckity* was she thinking, daring August like that? I'm sure he could tell how much I want him from the way I kissed him ...

Or maybe he couldn't. If he hasn't figured it out after all these years, maybe I'm in the clear. Maybe he thinks I'm just a good kisser—at least he said I am—and that's that.

Except ...

He didn't come over this morning the way he usually does. He hasn't texted me since his "Night" last night. A word that I've over-analyzed in every way. And while, sure, he said other things before that, it felt like an abrupt ending. Did he mean "Night" as in "Good night, don't worry, we're still friends"? Or "Night" as in "I don't know what the hell to do with you now that I've guessed you're a creepy creeper who creeps"? Or "Night" as in "Goodbye, you weirdo, have a good life."

Not that I'm catastrophizing and focusing on the worst possible scenario, dangit. But still, this little voice inside me wants to know if, with that one kiss, I ruined everything.

I'd putter around my house if there was anything to putter with, but everything is where it's supposed to be. Still, I have all this excess energy. Who do I talk to about my feelings for August, when he's the one I tell everything to? No one. I have no one to talk to.

That's not totally true. Danny would be safe. And maybe Sam. I know he keeps all sorts of secrets. He has to, dating a pop star.

Besides, everyone who was at One saw what happened, and I'm sure they're itching for an explanation.

What is August thinking? How can I get him to talk to me?

Exercise. As much as I'm not into it, maybe that can break the ice.

NOAH

Any interest in a bike ride

AUGUST

Are you seriously asking me

He has a point. I never initiate exercise.

NOAH

Yeah. If we're going to do the triathlon, we should train

AUGUST

I can't do it today. Have to run errands. Tomorrow's May's birthday.

But maybe Monday after work.

I let out a breath. If I keep thinking about this, I'm going to end up climbing the walls.

NOAH

Sure!

I groan. "Sure!"? I sound like I'm twelve. But he doesn't text me anything else the rest of the weekend.

* * *

Monday morning, I brainstorm with Sam about how to help the LGBTQIA+ lobbying group that recently hired us. They're looking for ways to expand housing for at-risk teens, and Sam knows just who to have them talk to. He sets up a meeting between his grandfather's office of policy and Stephen with a *ph* and Steven with a *v*. While that makes me feel accomplished, something is still very wrong in my life.

So as I pass reception midmorning, I wait until Shelby hangs up the phone before I blurt out, "August is acting weird."

Then I cringe, because I'm acting weird, too. Add that to acting like I'm twelve, and I'm a total mess.

Shelby doesn't react like I've said anything unusual. He straightens his shoulders, his bleached platinum hair falling into his dark eyes, and looks up at me and raises his eyebrows. "How so?"

I lean on the counter while Demi, our office manager, walks by. When the coast is clear, I whisper, "I don't know. He's not avoiding me, but he kind of is. And he's also just ... I can't put my finger on it."

"It was the kiss," Shelby says flatly.

I nod.

He sighs, leans over the counter, and tugs on my sleeve. "Can we talk? Let me see if Demi can cover the desk for a moment. Meet you in your office?"

"Sure." Shelby trots off to catch Demi, and I head to my office.

In a few moments, he swishes in and closes the door behind him.

"What do I do?" I groan. "What did I do wrong?"

"Oh, you did nothing wrong," Shelby purrs. "But you're obviously bothered by the fact that you got roped into kissing the love of your life."

My hopes sink to the floor. "Love of my life?"

He puts a hand on his slim hip. "Don't act surprised. Everyone in the office—with one notable exception—knows that you're in love with him."

Dang.

I blink.

I open my mouth, but he puts up his hand. "Yes, it's that obvious. There's an office pool as to how long it will take you guys to get together."

My heart starts thudding so fast I get scared I'm having a heart attack, and I begin pacing—apparently that's all I'm good at doing these days—and tugging at my hair with both hands. "No. No, no, no, no. This can't be happening. No one can know ... Oh my god. *He* can't know." I slide my hands down my face and groan, "Fuuuuck."

I try not to swear, but if there was ever a good time for it, it's now. Because if *everyone* knows ... then my life is ruined. He doesn't like me like that, and I'll lose him and my surrogate family and the firm I've created and all my friends ...

Shelby reaches up to touch my shoulder. He's shorter than me and very slight, but his comforting gesture makes him seem larger. "Hey," he says in a quieter voice. "Deep breaths. Let's sort this out."

I nod, and he points to a chair. I dutifully sit. Again, feeling like a twelve-year-old.

"Item number one," he says, holding up a tanned finger. "You're in love with your best friend, August Ramirez, and this is not something new."

I open my mouth to protest, out of habit, and he crosses his arms over his narrow chest, giving me a hard look. Letting out a sigh, I shake my head in defeat. "It's not new. I've been in love with him for a very long time."

Saying it out loud does something to me. My feelings for August are a rock I've been carrying around in my backpack for more than a decade. No one else could see it, but it's affected my every move.

Except maybe that rock poked out of the backpack—or at least made it lumpy enough so that other people suspected it was in there all along.

He uncrosses his arms and holds up another finger. "Item number two. For some reason, he did not seem to know this."

My first reaction is relief, but then the panic surges back, and I put a hand on each arm of the chair and go to stand. "He doesn't know. He *can't* know!"

"Shh." Shelby makes a downward motion with his hands. "I know you're scared. But let's walk through this."

"Okay," I mutter.

"Personally, I think he has deep feelings for you, too, but that's another story."

I'm losing track of how many times my heart soars and sinks in this conversation. But it's definitely soaring right now. "Why do you think that?"

"Because he does."

Anddd, sinking again. "That's not an answer."

"It is," he insists. "Let me continue?"

"Okay."

Shelby looks as satisfied as a cat drinking cream. He holds up another finger. "Item three. You changed things unintentionally by agreeing to that dare at One."

Despite my whirlwind of emotions and keyed-up state, I can't help smiling at the memory. "It was a nice kiss."

"Nice?"

"All right, it was amazing."

"It was really hot, Noah."

I nod. "Yeah. If I only get to kiss him once—well, once as an adult—at least it was a good one. Even if it was public as all hell."

"It was indeed. Public, that is. And good, too, at least from the way it looked." He fans himself. "Anyhow, while you have been secure in your feelings, unrequited though you fear they might be, for a while, he may have gotten a jolt to his system when he learned —no surprise to anyone else—that he liked kissing you."

"You think he did?"

Shelby coughs as he says, "Boner." Then he thumps his chest. "Yes, I think so."

"But ... *really*?" How could I not have noticed that?

"Yes, really."

I didn't notice because I was so deep in my feels. I slump back in the chair. "If it was a shock to him, should I let him off the hook? Tell him that the kiss didn't mean anything?"

Even though it meant *everything*.

Shelby eyes me dubiously. "Do you really think that's a good idea?"

"Do you have a better one?"

He tilts his head to the side exaggeratedly. "You could, you know, tell him how you feel."

I shake my head so vehemently I start to get a headache. "No. Absolutely not."

"I don't understand your reluctance. Anyone can see that August loves you, too."

"No, he doesn't. Not the way I love him. And I can't tell him because it would make everything awkward. It's always awkward when someone likes you more than you like them. I mean, I assume that's the way it goes. I don't actually know, since I've never experienced it, but I've seen enough teen comedies."

"Oh my god. Don't base your life on someone else's screenplay." Shelby shakes his finger at me like he's scolding a small child.

"You have to be a risk-taker. I mean, you already are. You started a firm straight out of law school instead of doing the safe thing, like taking a government job or grinding hours at a big law firm."

"True … but that's a *business* risk. I'm good with those."

"I assume August is, too, since you two are in business together."

"No, actually. I've had to push him every step of the way. Kind of like how he pushes me to do more physical activity than I care to. If it were up to him, we'd be jet skiing and spelunking and I don't know whatever else." I shiver. "No, thanks."

"But you let him talk you into doing the triathlon." It's not a question. August must've told him. Shelby sits back and tilts his head. "So you're a risk-taker with finances but not your body. He's a risk-taker with his body but not finances. And neither of you likes to take risks with your heart."

I stare at him. "You really are the eyes and ears of this firm."
Shelby shrugs.

"So what do I do, Shelbs? Is there anything *to* do? Is this something I just leave alone?"

"Ah, that's item number four. What do you do? I see two choices. You can continue as you have been, loving him up close and yet so far away. Or you can tell him."

"And risk rejection and making things awkward for our friendship and also our business partnership."

"Which is why you don't want to tell him unless you know what his feelings are for sure."

I shrug. "Basically. I mean, this has been the status quo my entire life, practically. At least since puberty. I'd rather be around him and get to spend time with him, even if it's not in the way I want."

He nods. "Okay. Then maybe I need to dig around a bit—"
"No. Absolutely not."
"What if I do it slyly?"

"You're as sly as a cat being startled by a cucumber."

Shelby rolls his eyes. "I can be coy if I want to." He sighs. "Look. I respect you, and I respect your boundaries, but even though you're my boss, I also consider you my friend. I want to see if I can find out how he feels about you. If I can do it in a low-key way, will that be all right? Not, like, some grand plan."

Record scratch. I glare. "You totally have a grand plan."

"I'll be good. I promise." How can someone who looks so angelic be so devious?

I scrub my face. "Fine. Okay. I don't think I can talk you out of this, and I'm not sure what else to do. I can't just ask him, 'Hey, August, did you see the light when our lips touched?' That's not going to work."

"But you want to know how he feels."

"Yeah," I admit. "I do."

"Then let me work my magic."

"Just don't make me regret it."

"I won't mess it up. I promise."

"Why do those feel like famous last words?"

"Because they might be." He grins at me before getting serious. "Hey. I'm not at all making fun of your feelings. I know how hard this has been for you, because I see you every day. It's obvious how much you care for him. And he's too oblivious to notice. But if there's a chance things could work out for you two, I'd love to help that along."

"Fine. Just don't make them worse." I let out a breath. "So what do I do in the meantime?"

"He's your best friend. Listen to him. Talk to him. Enjoy being with him. Run your business. Set your feelings aside for a little bit until this shakes out. I'm hoping he'll come to his senses and ask you out, but he might not."

"That's what I'm afraid of."

"Let me see what I can dig up. I'll be discreet." He pats my arm. "I know I can be gossipy, but it's because I love working here and I want everyone to be happy."

"I know." I give him a smile. "I'd better get back to work."

"Me, too."

But it's hard to concentrate on work, because I'm scared to death what he's going to find out.

CHAPTER 6

August

"Have you seen Noah today?" I ask Shelby when I get to the office Monday afternoon after court. I was running around all weekend long—running from my feelings about the kiss Noah and I shared, for sure. But now that I'm here, I might as well find out what's going on. And I want a heads-up before I go talk with Noah.

Shelby is everyone's friend and the office confidant. He has a spot-on ability to assess people and will deliver what they need. Whether it's a hug to a colleague who's down, ultraprofessional behavior to our prickliest client, or something in the middle.

He also cares deeply about this firm and what goes on in it. I think because it's a safe place—for him and for others. Since he's small and twinkish, he got teased in high school, but here we celebrate individuals being themselves. If Shelby wants to wear sparkly pink eye shadow and a skirt, that's fine. Most of the time, though, he can be found in a slim Polo shirt and slacks.

Something's up with Noah today, judging by the way Shelby doesn't meet my eyes. "Yes." He shifts in his chair.

"Why do you look guilty?"

Shelby raises his eyebrows and adopts a mock-offended, innocent expression. "What do you mean?"

"You know everything that's going on around here. And your usual answer when someone asks if you've seen one of the other attorneys is a lot more informative than 'yes' or 'no.' Is something up with Noah?"

After a brief hesitation, Shelby says, "Yeah."

"Then what is it?"

He rubs his face in frustration, then looks around shiftily before answering, voice low. "Look, August. I think Noah is *how he always is.*"

"What's that supposed to mean?"

"He's your best friend, right?" I nod. "So if you're concerned something's wrong, maybe you should ask him."

Annoyance flares through me, because he's giving me the runaround. I know he's only protecting Noah, but that's my job. "You just told me two different things," I say, my tone accusatory. "That he's fine, and that something is wrong."

He blinks his large brown eyes. "I didn't say either of those. And what I said is true. *Noah is how he always is.*" He says this with emphasis, like it's supposed to mean something, but I don't get it.

"That's not helpful." I sigh. "Something happened after we went to One?"

"No ..." Again, he says it as if there's more to his meaning than the word itself.

"So, the kiss." Might as well say it. It's been driving me up the wall. "Did he talk to you about it?"

"Even if he did, I'm not the one who matters."

I sigh. "I should just go talk to Noah."

"Yes, you should," Shelby says. But he puts out a hand to stop me. "Look, August. Have you ever considered dating him?"

"Of course," I say. "Or—I would. Except he doesn't like me like that."

He stares at me, his jaw dropping. "Why on earth would you say that? I mean, I understand that you fooled around a million years ago when you were experimenting as teens, and it didn't work, but I think anyone who was at the club Friday night knows that's no longer an issue. Why would you think he doesn't like you?"

"Because he said so."

Shelby waves a hand. "Pfft. That I find hard to believe."

The memory stings, but I lower my voice and tell him anyway. "When we were in high school, I … I kind of liked him. A lot. Even though things were so horrible and awkward that one time we messed around. And I was about to ask him out, see if maybe that had just been a fluke, but then I heard him talking to another kid. He didn't deny being gay, but he said he didn't like me that way. He said he wasn't attracted to me." I shrug, trying to be nonchalant. "So I took him at his word. I figured he meant it and we were better as friends."

Shelby's mouth drops open. "Is that why you've never considered dating Noah? Because you thought he didn't want you?"

I tilt my head to think about it. "I guess so. I mean, when someone says flat out that they aren't interested in you, you tend to think it's a nonstarter, right? On top of not even being able to get off with each other. Sorry, didn't mean to be TMI."

"All good."

"Well, between his words and actions, I wasn't going to try to change his mind, especially when I liked him so much as a friend."

"But back then, you were interested? You thought he was cute?"

"More than cute. Hot as fuck. I've always been attracted to Noah. It's a constant, like the ocean has tides." I gaze at Shelby. "So … do you still think I should talk to him?"

He throws up his hands. "Yes."

I sigh. "Fine." Right then, my phone buzzes. Thoughtlessly, I'd set it on the reception desk.

Shelby reaches to hand it to me. "Noooo," I say, shooting a hand out and grabbing it, but it's too late. He's seen the name of the person who texted me, and he can see the GIF on the lock screen.

"What the hell? Noah sends you porn?" Comprehension dawns on his face. "Is that what you two are always texting back and forth?"

I groan. "Yes. It's a game we have. It's not sexual." I cringe. "Well, it is, but it's meant to be a joke."

He gives me a skeptical look. "Hmm."

"What's that supposed to mean?"

Shelby shrugs. "Most people don't sext people they only think of platonically."

"We're not sexting."

"Fine. In any case, you should go talk with him."

"Thanks," I mutter, and I stroll off feeling utterly confused. That conversation was unenlightening, to say the least.

I find Noah in his office, staring at his computer. I give him my biggest smile as I tap on the doorjamb, and he looks up, startled, then composes himself as usual. He returns my grin, but I study it for any issues.

He looks like the same Noah Weston as always.

"Hey," I say. I come in and close the door behind me, then sit in one of his chairs.

He tilts his head in confusion, his gray-blue eyes mesmerizing. "What's up?"

I thread my fingers together. "Dunno. You tell me."

Noah frowns and looks all around. Seeing nothing, he turns to me. "Wh-what are you talking about?"

"It seems like something's off with you. Is something on your mind? I'm your best friend. I'm supposed to know these things."

He swallows. "There's nothing new going on. I'm just thinking about some old stuff."

"That counts. Whatever is bothering you counts."

"I guess ... I have feelings for someone, but they aren't returned."

This comes as a surprise to me, and it gives me a slight stomachache. "I didn't know you liked someone."

Noah shrugs. "Yeah. I do. But it can't go anywhere."

"Can I guess who it is?"

And why does it make me pissed that Noah might like someone? He's allowed.

Except.

Except, I might be wanting him for myself.

"I really don't want you to guess," he says.

Well, now I'm offended. "Why not?"

Noah looks defeated. "Because whether you know who it is or not, it's not going to change anything."

"What if I talk to him for you. Tell him you're a great guy."

Why the fuck am I offering this? Why, why?

"I don't think that will help. Either someone likes you, or they don't. You know?"

"I just don't want you to ... hurt," I say. "I care about you."

"Thanks," Noah says. He turns his focus to his computer, but I can't leave him like this. I need to get back to spending time with him.

"Meet you at five thirty?" I blurt. "To go biking?"

I'm very carefully not asking Noah if he wants to kiss again. I'm not asking him if he thinks about me in any sexual way. We're keeping this on friend topics.

"Sounds good. But for now, you should get to work."

"Whatever, boss." I smile at him and take off.

While we exercise together and see each other at the office, the rest of the week still sucks. Even though we talk, I feel like something's wrong, and I don't know what it is.

* * *

On Thursday evening, I'm at another family party at my abuelita's in Echo Park.

My family has parties just about every week. It's always someone's birthday or someone is graduating or it's Mother's Day or Father's Day. Or, hell, there's a funeral. Whatever. There's always something going on, and if there isn't, someone will make something up. We see each other all the time.

The place isn't particularly huge, but it's set up to handle a crowd—a crowd of people happy to sit on folding chairs and use tables from Costco in the backyard.

In this family, we don't really have secrets. People ask you your business at the dinner table, and I grew up knowing that I needed to just say whatever was on my chest and not keep it bottled up.

Except tonight, as I sit and drain my beer, I look around and feel like I'm on the outside for the first time.

I can't tell them that what I'm feeling toward my best friend is starting to change, because what if I have it wrong? I don't want to get their hopes up—especially since Noah's apparently interested in someone else. And god knows all of my aunts would call him up or corner him the next time he comes over if they knew I liked him, and then I'd have to move to another state.

As much as I complain about my tías, I know they love me. Just, sometimes I don't feel like explaining myself.

I've avoided them so far by roping my tío Raymond into talking with me. Raymond's a handsome guy with dark hair turning gray at the temples. He's my mom's oldest brother, and he's been out as long as I can remember. I've learned two things from him: to be myself, and to not let things get me down.

But if I thought chatting with him would get me out of talking about Noah, I was very wrong. He hands me a fresh beer and asks, "Where's your other half?"

I furrow my brows. "You mean Dos?"

"Yeah. Did you bring him?" Tío Raymond looks around.

I swallow. "No, not tonight."

"Was he busy?"

What's with all the questions? My voice comes out sharp. "I don't know. I didn't ask him."

Now it's my uncle's turn to look confused. "Wait. Is something wrong? Did you guys have a falling-out?"

"No, nothing like that. We don't always have to do everything together. Sheesh."

"All right, all right." He holds his hands up. "Don't get defensive. I was just asking. You have to admit it's rare for you two to be separated."

I blow out a breath. "Yeah, that's true. But I think he's seeing someone I don't know about. Or at least … he said he liked someone who didn't like him as much. The whole situation pisses me off."

A wrinkle forms in my uncle's forehead. "Are you … jealous?"

I pause and think about it. "I mean, you know. Maybe?"

Tío Raymond leans forward. "Interesting. Does the thought of him with someone else make you upset?"

"Very." It makes me see red.

"Then you need to tell him how you feel."

I stare at him. First Shelby, now Tío Raymond. I may have trouble getting things through my thick head sometimes, but is the answer that easy?

It wasn't before, because I didn't know what my feelings were. Now I know: I have a thing for my best friend.

Fuck it. I don't need to wait for a third person to tell me. I don't spend time contemplating life. I prefer to take action.

Even if I could get hurt.

I set down my drink. "Okay. I'mma go do that."

He chuckles and leans back in his chair. "I didn't mean now— Okay. You're going. See you later."

If he says anything else, I don't hear it. I'm racing to my car.

CHAPTER 7

Noah

There's a pounding on my door late Thursday night. I've been sitting watching a TV show and contemplating my life choices, wondering if I should get ready for bed. As I walk up to the door, I hear, "Noah, I know you're in there."

I open the door to a wild-eyed August. "Hey," I say, worried and wary. "How come you didn't use your key like you usually do? What's wrong?"

"I don't know," he says, pacing around my living room and pulling his hair. He's acting the way I have been all week. "I'm going out of my skin, and I can't talk to anyone about it. It's the kind of thing I'd talk to you about, but I can't talk to you about it because you're my best friend, but fuck it. I'm doing it. What the hell was up with that kiss?"

Well, August. What was up with it is, I'm in love with you.

But I have to let him off the hook. "Mes, it was just a kiss." I smile, trying for reassurance, but it probably comes across as pretty weak.

He stares at me. "Is that really all it was for you?"

I'm tempted to lie and say yes, but I won't do that. So I deflect. "What was it for you?"

August stops pacing and plants himself right in front of me. I take a step back. "Answer the question." His voice is low and husky.

I brace myself for the possibility of losing him.

"No, it wasn't just a kiss," I say to my feet. Then I look into his eyes. "You mean a lot to me. Even more than being my best friend. Once we started kissing, I couldn't hide my feelings for you, and I've been going back and forth all week trying to figure out how to tell you how much I want you. In all the ways. So, yeah, it wasn't just a kiss. It meant more—"

August interrupts me by slamming me against a wall and kissing me. Hard. He attacks me with his soft lips and insistent tongue.

I grunt, at first shocked, and then I kiss him back as fervently as he's kissing me.

God. Yes. Kissing August. I can smell his soap and the laundry detergent he uses. He tastes faintly of beer and pot, but mostly he tastes like August—and it's simultaneously familiar and sexy.

I should protest. Not because I don't want to be kissing him—I *so* want to be kissing him—but because I know that once we get our hormones or whatever out of the way, there could be fallout.

Except I can't bring myself to care about that in this moment.

Gripping his hips, I tug him to me, and he reaches for my face, cradling my cheeks and pulling me closer.

This kiss is wild. It's like someone pressed a little button, but a massive explosion went off. Because it's not just me that can't get enough of him. It seems like he can't get enough of me, either, and that's ... amazing.

Since I might be dreaming, I try to memorize every sensation —the sound of his groans, the pressure of his chest against mine. What his ass feels like under my hands, because he's muscled, and it's firm.

When we break apart, both breathing hard, we look into each other's eyes but are kissing again before we can say anything. It's like we're scared to break the spell. This moment is magic, and we don't want the bubble to burst. This kiss is all the dreams I've ever had in my entire life coming true in less than a minute.

Eventually things slow down, and we end up almost sipping from each other. Taking and giving languid kisses that meet and break apart and then surge back together again like waves.

I've hardened fast, and he was already hard, and we're rubbing our erections together. The zipper of my jeans is chafing me, but I can't bring myself to care about that, either.

I want the pain. I want the pleasure. I want to feel like I'm alive and things are going to go my way.

"It was fucking more than a kiss, and you know it," August growls against my skin, and my whole body shivers in a way I've never experienced before. "We care about each other. I don't know what this is or what we're doing, but that kiss changed everything. I can't even look at anyone else. I don't see anyone but you. I want you. Do you have any idea how sexy you are?"

I shake my head.

"And I wanted you before," he murmurs. "I just didn't know you felt the same way."

"I do."

"Then get naked."

I have a better idea, so I push him back by the shoulders. At first he looks hurt, but then I drop to my knees in front of him, and he groans.

"Let me," I whisper. "Please."

"Fuck, Dos, you on your knees. You're a wet dream."

"You've dreamed about me?"

He shrugs and his expression goes sheepish, and it makes my heart throb. Other parts, too.

But it doesn't distract me from the job at hand. I undo his pants and take out his hard dick, and gosh. I want it. I want him.

His brown skin and tip are swollen, with veins protruding. I suck and lick his hairless balls as I shove his pants and underwear down to his knees.

He groans and rips at my hair, almost too hard. Except it's not. It's perfect.

I lick up the base of his thick cock, and he says, "Stop fucking teasing me, Dos—"

I swallow him down.

He's big, and I'm not the best at deep throating, but I can do it for a few moments.

August whimpers. He actually frigging whimpers, and a big rush of power surges through me at the realization that I can make him feel that good.

I start to gag, so I ease off to rest, then start sucking on the tip of his cock.

"Oh god," he says. "You look fucking … Oh god, yes, please."

I pause again and look up at him through my lashes. He cradles my face gently, and the soft look on his face almost makes me tear up. Because, jeez, he's directing that attention at me. The way I've always wanted him to.

"Want to come?" I ask.

"Yeah," he says roughly. "Not yet, though. Just … take off your clothes," he says, his voice commanding. And it does something to me. I've never heard him sound like that.

I stand up, but instead of getting undressed, I shove his shirt up and yank it over his head. He chuckles and steps out of the rest of his clothes.

Then August Ramirez is standing in front of me, totally naked, and I really should be back on my knees. But before I can move, he leans forward and kisses me, and I grab his ass, squeezing it and letting him rut into me. His hands are all over my back, and I realize that he's lifting up my shirt. We break apart long enough for me to shed my clothes.

And this is the first time since high school that we've been body to body with no clothes on.

We do this little shuffle dance, not wanting to let go of each other, still kissing, but wanting to get somewhere other than my entryway. I grab his hand. "Come on."

In my bedroom, we fall down on the bed and get tangled up in each other. We stroke and kiss, tongues as interlaced as our legs.

We're diagonal, so I turn us so our heads are on the pillows, and he laughs. "Always need to be lined up like utensils in a drawer?"

"Yeah."

Our kisses go from frenzied to deeper. From frantic and almost violent to long, hard caresses.

"Do you want to fuck me?" I ask.

He sits back on his heels and studies my face. "Yeah?"

"You asking or telling me?"

"I'm asking if it's all right."

"It's more than all right."

"I want to fuck you," he says. "But I don't know about tonight. Feels like a lot of pressure." He looks away. "And I don't want it to be bad for you."

"It could never be bad if it's with you. We've learned a lot since we were teenagers. You know what you're doing now, and so do I."

He looks down. "Maybe not."

I blink. "What?"

"I haven't fucked as many people as you think I have."

"What have you been doing all this time, then?"

"Well, I go out, but sometimes I'll ditch the date early and go work out or something." He blushes. "I don't hook up anywhere near as much as it seems."

I stare at him, reflecting on what he's told me in the past. He hasn't ever lied to me, I don't think. I just assumed he was doing things he wasn't. "You're not a virgin, are you?"

He laughs. "No, but it's been so long I may as well be."

I am flabbergasted. Here I thought my best friend was a player, like Danny, but he's more innocent, like Danny's boyfriend Alden. Except without the shyness.

"So let's hold off on that," I say. "Hand jobs?"

He nods. "Sounds good."

"Let me get some lube. Hang on." I lean over, and he pinches my bare ass. I swat him, but then he leans down and bites my cheek, and I groan, rutting my dick into the bed. "Christ, August. I had no idea you were into biting."

"After all the porn I've sent you, you have no idea what I'm into."

I pour some lube into my hand. "I didn't know if you were looking for weird positions or if you thought it was hot or what."

"Kind of both. Some of it is weird. Most of it is hot. I want to try a lot of it."

"With who?"

"Well, if you're up for it," he starts.

And my heart stops. "Are you saying ... What are you saying? Do you want to have a lot of sex with me? Because that's what I want. I mean, with you."

He smiles against my skin. "Yes." My lubed-up hand meets his hard cock, and he groans. "Fuck, you feel so good. Let me."

He slicks up his hand and starts stroking my cock.

And this feels even more intimate. Because we're chest to chest. Lip to lip, kissing. Except we keep pausing to watch while we stroke each other. We're each savoring the other's reaction while at the same time enjoying the pleasure, and it's this awesome feedback loop that I wish would go on forever.

But it's going to end, because I'm about to come. I tell him so, and he grins against my mouth. "Me, too."

In a few more strokes, I let go of his dick as my climax hits. He takes control, jerking himself hard and fast over me.

His face transforms with his release, and the sight is compelling enough that it distracts me from my own orgasm. When he opens his eyes, he gives me a sheepish smile and then runs a finger through the mess he's left on my chest.

"Sorry," he whispers.

"Don't be. It was hot." I tug him to me, not willing to let things get awkward, and we kiss again.

We kiss like we're lovers. Like we've been lovers for a very long time.

I don't want to talk, and I can tell that he doesn't know what to say. So after a while, I take his hand, and he comes quietly with me to the bathroom, where I turn on the shower. Once the water is warm, we both step in, still not talking, but kissing a lot. And we wash each other off.

When we're dry, I pull him back to bed. He raises an eyebrow. We've slept together plenty—literally slept—though never naked.

But he doesn't object. He just gets in behind me and wraps me up in his arms. Soon enough, I feel his breathing go heavy. My breathing softens, and then I'm asleep, too.

CHAPTER 8

August

I wake up next to Noah. It's not the first time that's happened, but it feels different, because of what we did last night.

My arm's flung over his torso, because he's mine.

Noah's fucking *mine*.

I want to go make him some coffee, but I also don't want to move. I must've jostled him, because he turns toward me and yawns, then opens his eyes all sleepy and sweet. He blinks a few times before he focuses on me and smiles, and something about that smile makes my heart melt.

"Good morning," he says.

"Hey." I roll him onto his back and kiss him before he can do anything else.

All that glorious naked skin underneath me, and he's hard. He kisses me back languidly, and it feels like we have all our lives to explore one another.

I don't want to break the spell. When I came over last night, I had to have him, and nothing's changed since then. If anything, it's gotten more intense, because I know what he tastes like and the noises he makes. I know how sexy he is when he's about to come, and how giving he is. He made me feel like I was the most important person in the world last night.

I'm going to do the same for him right now.

My hand slips down between us, and I grip his length. He gasps into my kisses, and I proceed to wake him up thoroughly.

* * *

After we've showered and we're sitting at Noah's breakfast table, I can't handle not knowing where we stand. I blurt out, "So, what are we doing? Are we now friends with benefits? Or what?"

Noah sets down his coffee and studies me. I'm not used to him looking at me this way. Finally, he swallows. "Is that what you want?"

I shrug. "I mean, you're my best friend forever, only now we're ... or rather, we could ... um. Well, we could be friends and also have sex."

He looks down at his feet.

"Hey," I say. "What's wrong?"

"I'm just trying to sort out my thoughts."

The light dawns, and jealousy spikes through me. "Is it that other guy you're seeing? If we're going to be friends with benefits, I want to be exclusive."

Noah's cheek twitches. "I'm not seeing anyone."

"You said there was someone you liked—"

He leans forward and puts a hand on mine. "It was *you*."

I blink. "Me?"

He chuckles without humor. "Yes, Mes. I like you."

"Oh. Well. Hmm. I like you, too." I scrub my face. "Look, if this is going to mess us up, we don't have to."

"Do you think that this will mess us up?"

"Nah. It's just sex." Except it feels like that's the wrong thing to say. I hasten to add, "I think that's the way to look at it. Because we've been best friends forever. We can continue to be best friends in the future. Just now we fuck sometimes."

"I'm hoping more than sometimes," Noah says wryly, and I laugh.

"Fair enough." But he still looks worried. "Hey," I say. "You know I'll always be here for you."

He gulps. "Yeah. Same."

"So what's the big deal? We don't have to do this if you don't want to."

"No big deal. It's fine."

"We just kind of fell into bed. And I don't know. I don't normally chat about that kind of thing. But I can't ignore it with you. I have to be sure I don't lose you. Because I can't." I squeeze his hand. "You've gotten me through so much. We have so much history together. I don't want to throw it away because we couldn't keep our dicks in our pants."

"No," he says. "I don't think we'll be throwing it away."

I smile. "So ... friends with benefits?"

"Yeah. Although—dang. I'm such a lawyer sometimes. I want to know what the definition of that is. Does it mean we kiss?"

I lean in and kiss him, and, after a beat, he kisses me back. It seems I've surprised him. And then we kiss some more.

I can't get enough of kissing Noah.

When we finally break apart, I'm aroused and I can tell he is, too.

"So, okay. Kissing is good." He licks his swollen lips.

"And I'm good with doing anything I've ever sent you or you've ever sent me in a GIF," I say.

His eyes bug open. "That doesn't leave much off the table."

I grin and take my coffee cup into the kitchen.

* * *

After a few hours at work, I slide into Noah's office like I'm sliding into his DMs, and before he can get up, I lean over his desk and kiss him.

He kisses back after a second, and when I withdraw, he chases my lips like we're magnetized.

We kind of are.

Then he blinks. "Did you come in here just to kiss me?"

I chuckle. "Um. Yes. Obviously."

"*Why*?"

I give him a cocky grin and shrug. "I felt like it. Is that okay?"

He frowns, and my heart sinks. Because maybe we're not on the same page about this after all. "I guess. I mean, in general, yes, but I don't know about doing it in the office. It feels like we're muddling things up. I know what to do around you when you're my best friend. But now that, um ..."

"Now that we've seen each other naked—"

"We've done that before—"

"Now that we've seen each other come a few times. Recently."

He nods. "That."

"You're so cute," I blurt. "We send each other all those sex GIFs, and yet you can barely talk about it."

Noah glares at me. "I can talk about anything, thankyouverymuch. I just don't necessarily want to talk about it at work, where anyone can overhear us."

That makes me feel a little ... rebuffed. Does Noah feel it's inappropriate? Is he ashamed? Are we too new?

I don't want to know the answer to those questions, at least not yet. "That's fair." I squeeze his shoulder. "We can talk about things later."

I turn and walk away.

* * *

When our group goes to One that evening, I don't know how to act. I really want to hold Noah and kiss him, but does this still fall under his "not at work" rule?

Alice eyes us warily, but she's serving a different section, so we aren't close enough for her to interrogate us. It ends up being a nice night. I dance with Danny and Alden while Noah talks with Charlie and his sister Reyna, who are also attorneys at our office. The siblings brought their brother Camden, who Shelby eyes up and down—but I think Cam is straight.

At the end of the night, Noah and I exit, sweaty and laughing, trading the loud music of the bar for the quieter night. It's like walking into a vacuum.

Because we'd found on-street parking—a rarity—we have a bit of a hike ahead of us. We bypass the valet and take a shortcut down the alley that runs behind One.

"What was up with you and that little dancer dude?" Noah asks.

"Nothing. Just dancing."

The alley smells like trash cans and piss. Charming.

"Seemed like you were having fun," he says.

"Are you jealous?" I ask, teasing. I give his shoulder a gentle shove.

"What? No," he scoffs. He shoves me back, and I wrap my arms around him to get him in a kind of headlock.

For most of our lives, we're been pretty evenly matched, although lately I've been working out more. But he gets the advantage by slipping out and coming up behind me to hop on my back, wrapping his arms around me and pinning my arms to my sides.

I laugh and stumble toward the nearest wall, then turn around, mashing Noah against the bricks. Not hard. Just a bit of roughhousing.

Once his feet hit the ground, he retaliates, lunging toward me. Laughing, I push him with both hands, then step toward him and lean in for a quick kiss.

He blinks. I grin. I've confused him.

But then it's my turn to be confused as he reaches a hand behind my neck and draws me to him. And we're kissing again, tongues clashing, then gentling.

It's a kiss where we're battling, then calling a truce. Then another attack and another truce. Over and over, and it's not long before we're both hard.

"Fuck," he whispers, and part of me cheers that I made him swear.

"Do you want to stop?" I gasp.

"No."

"Can I suck you off?"

He stumbles. Then he nods.

The alley is dirty, but no one's back here, and I'm pretty sure it's not the first time someone's gotten head in the shadows behind this club.

I drop to my knees and yank his pants down, releasing his hard cock. I don't give myself time to admire him, knowing I have to make this fast. I go to town, sucking as hard as I can. While I have a gag reflex, I can usually stave it off if I don't go too deep.

"Jeez, Mes. You look so hot doing that. I'm gonna come."

That's the idea, I think, but I don't stop what I'm doing to say it. I want to keep the rhythm going, steady and drawing him out.

He's writhing and moaning, and soon he shouts as he comes in my mouth, warm and bitter and salty.

I made Noah come again.

I keep him in my mouth, wanting to keep him sheltered, wanting to prolong the connection. But when he pulls away, I help him tuck himself back in. I get to my feet and lean in to kiss him. He returns the kiss distractedly, then cups my erection.

"You don't have to," I mutter.

"I want to."

"The longer we stay here, the more likely we are to get caught for public indecency."

"Then you'd better come fast."

And now Noah is kneeling in front of me, and I understand what he was feeling a few minutes ago. I see how hot this is, because while I love the act of giving, this kind of indulgence is unbelievably sexy, too.

Noah appears to not have a gag reflex. He's deep throating me—no one else has ever done that to me—and I'm wondering where the fuck he learned how.

I'm loving it, though.

I hear two people talking, and it scares me into paying attention to my surroundings. I need to finish quick or we're going to get caught, and it's pretty easy to focus on finishing because damn, Noah can suck cock. It's not just his skills, though. It's the way he's so into it. All his attention is on me, and it's such a rush.

Being from such a big family, I'm not used to that kind of focus. It's a big deal.

But before I get too philosophical, I near my climax, and Noah pushes me up and over with a few more sucks aided by his hands.

I slump against the brick wall and do my best to pull my pants up so my wet, soft dick is out of view.

Noah stands, brushing off his knees, and I pull him to me, hugging him hard. At first, he seems surprised by my embrace, but he catches on, clinging to me just as strongly.

"Hey," I whisper. "You're amazing. Don't forget that."

He nods into my chest. "You, too."

I pull back enough to see his face and give him a gentle kiss that goes on too long. Soon we hear footsteps and catcalls, and I recognize Danny's voice. Noah and I break apart sheepishly.

"So, like, is this a thing now?" Danny asks, gesturing between us. He has his arm slung around Alden, who's grinning up at him like Danny is his entire world.

I shrug and glance at Noah, who's shrugging, too.

"Um, yeah. I think so," I say, looking to Dos for reassurance.

He smiles and holds my hand. "We're still best friends," he tells Danny.

But "best friends" doesn't seem like the right term.

CHAPTER 9

Noah

August kisses me at my front door but then excuses himself to sleep in his own bed, claiming that he needs to get up early to go see his grandma. I can't help being disappointed, but I know that August and I aren't like that, all couple-like. Sure, for years we've ended up sleeping on top of or next to each other often enough, but now that we're something more ... it's weird.

Anyway, I need to visit my grandfather in the morning. And one night apart won't hurt us. Right?

I feel gross from the club, so I take a rinse-off shower and climb into bed. It's super late, but I'm restless and can't sleep.

"What have I done?" I say to the ceiling. Because I don't have anyone else to say it to.

Funnily enough, the ceiling doesn't answer. Jerk.

I'm not entirely sure what I'm asking, though. Perhaps, is being friends with benefits even going to work when I want romance and love?

I've wanted August for so long, I can't think of what it was like to *not* want him. In fact, I don't think I've ever wanted anyone other than him.

Throughout the years, the guys I've dated have been sort of placeholders for August. I've had relationships, but they've always felt superficial.

Now that I have him, though, I'm full of questions. Do I *really* have him? Is best friends with benefits different from being boyfriends? Does it even matter?

I fall into a restless sleep, and too early, my alarm wakes me up.

* * *

I check in with the front desk at the care facility, then walk down the hall that smells of antiseptic to room 203. I brace myself before I poke my nose through the door.

Most of the time, Grandpa's lucid, but the days when he's not are tough. Sometimes I feel like I have deep wells of patience to deal with the changes he can't control, and other times, not so much. But it really gets to me when he doesn't recognize me.

Because if he's my only family who actually loves me, and he doesn't know me, then do I exist anymore?

Okay, I'm being dramatic. My mom loves me. She just ... doesn't feel like she needs to worry about me. It's like she figured I was strong enough to fend for myself, so her work was done.

Thing is, I don't want to fend for myself a lot of the time. Maybe that's why I like being around August so much. He takes care of me. Although I suppose it goes both ways.

"Noah!" Grandpa calls, and I step in, letting out a breath. It's already a plus if he remembers who I am.

"Hey, Grandpa! Good to see you!"

I give him a hug and sit down next to him. He's sitting up in his wheelchair, the television on volume one million. I turn it down to just slightly too loud.

"Where's August?" he asks.

"He went to see his grandmother today."

Grandpa nods sagely. "He's a good one, that August. You picked a good boyfriend."

"He's not my boyfriend, Grandpa. He's my best friend."

"Why do you say he's not your boyfriend? I thought you two were sweeties."

I shake my head sadly. "I mean, no? I don't know. We're not like that." I can't imagine calling August my "sweetie." Or vice versa.

"He treats you well, though?"

"Of course. He always has."

"Good. I wouldn't want you to settle for anything less than what you are worth." He rolls his eyes. "My daughter never understood that."

"I know."

"She seems to think that she can find her value in someone else. But she can't. She needs to be enough for herself."

I sit back in the chair. "While that's true, I still want a boyfriend, you know?"

"Is that ever going to be August?"

"Sheesh, Grandpa, ask the tough questions when I've only had one cup of coffee."

He smiles. "We could talk about the food here if you like."

I shake my head and think about how cool it is that I can talk to him about my love life (or lack thereof). I remember his gentle reaction to my sexuality so many years ago.

I'm fifteen years old and hunched over my desk in my room, the music on my headphones turned up as loud as I can stand, so I miss the knock on the door. In fact, I miss the door opening, him stepping inside, everything, until my grandfather is standing in front of me, a concerned look on his face.

Quickly, I remove the headphones and look up at him, wiping the tears from my face.

I don't fool him.

He squats down in front of me. "Hey."

I swallow hard. "Hey."

"I'm sorry you had to hear that conversation." He shakes his head. "Your mother can sure pick 'em sometimes."

My stomach knots. Because what if her boyfriend is right? What if I am a gross little fairy?

Getting tired of crouching down, Grandpa parks himself on the edge of the bed across from me. "Noah, I need you to know something."

I can't get my voice to work. I see red sparks behind my eyes, and I have a headache, and I'm just so, so tired. Because he's going to tell me I have to leave. And then I'll have no place to go. Not unless August lets me move in, but he already has so many sisters.

I'm so lost in my thoughts, I miss what Grandpa says next. I blink at him, and he smiles.

"I said, it's okay if you're gay."

His words hit me at a soul-deep level, and now the tears fall freely. "But she said ... and he said ..."

"They're wrong."

I blink. Then I burst into loud sobs, the kind of crying I haven't done since I was a tiny kid and fell down, scraping my knees. "I thought you were going to kick me out if you knew."

"No, bud. You're never getting kicked out of my home. I love you exactly the way you are, no matter who you're attracted to." He shrugs. "Besides, I already figured you weren't into girls."

My sobs pause because my jaw drops. "How?"

"Just a feeling I had." He gives me a kind smile, which turns to a frown. "I don't know what your mother's thinking. I mean, clearly, she's not thinking, dating that intolerant, insufferable ..." He shakes his head. Afternoon sunlight shines on his face, illuminating his wrinkled cheeks, and I couldn't love him more.

"I was scared," I whisper. "Because since Mom left me here, I thought if you don't approve of me ..."

"I'll always approve of you. Dontcha put your pants on one leg at a time?"

I chuckle. "Yeah."

"So do I. That means you're all right with me. Don't forget, it's you and me and Grandma, bud. We're family." He pats the bed next to him, and I sit by his side. He wraps an arm around my shoulder. "August is family, too."

"Yeah." I press my face to my grandpa's chest. "Do you think I should tell him? I mean, about me?"

"Yes, I do. You two are honest with each other, aren't you?"

I pause, because am I? I try to tell August everything, but there are a few things I've kept from him. Instead, I ask, "Do you think he'll ... Do you think he'll be mad? I mean, that I haven't told him?"

Grandpa pauses a moment. Then he says, "I think his response may surprise you. Don't wait. Get it over with."

I nod and go into the bathroom to wash my face before August comes over.

My mom dated my dad only long enough to get pregnant. Since him, she's been looking for the right one, never staying with anyone very long. But lately it's gotten worse. The new guy, Greg, doesn't hide his distaste for me, so I don't even see my mom very much anymore at all. But at least I have Grandma and Grandpa.

And hopefully August.

Later that same night, I'm sitting in my bedroom with my best friend, just kind of hanging out. "August?" I say. I can't keep the tremble out of my hands or the sick feeling from the pit of my stomach.

He looks up from his phone. "Yeah?" Seeing my expression, he sets his phone down and stares. "What's up? Are you okay?"

I shake my head. "I feel like I'm going to be sick."

"Want me to call your grandma?"

"No," I say quickly. "Not that kind of sick. I just wanted to tell you something. And if it makes you not my friend, I understand."

I don't actually understand. I'll die.

"Okay," he says slowly. "What's going on?"

"IthinkI'mgay." I say it as one word, but he gets the idea.

A big grin forms on his face. "Man, I kinda guessed that. I was hoping I wasn't the only one."

"Only one?"

"I think I might be bisexual."

This knot in my stomach unties and all the tension I'd been feeling just evaporates. "You do? I mean, you are?"

"Yeah. I dunno. I guess I didn't think it was that big a deal. My tío Raymond is gay."

"Oh." I smile weakly. "Cool."

I think, on some level, I might have figured August would accept me. But I couldn't be sure. When my own mother doesn't … it's just hard to know who to trust.

"Right? He's the best. He's taught me so much."

I stare at August, suddenly suspicious. "Speaking of Tío Raymond … do you happen to have any idea what happened to my soap?"

August starts cracking up. He holds his belly and can't stop laughing.

"What?" I ask. "Oh my god, you do. What did you do?"

"Borrowed my tía's clear nail polish and painted the whole thing. It was Raymond's idea. He's full of pranks."

"I was wondering why my Irish Spring wasn't very sudsy," I grumble.

August is still laughing hard, and I join him. I figured he had something to do with my shower troubles. He always has some prank to play on me, and many were inspired by his uncle's suggestions. I've learned over the years how to play his game, though.

"Is that why you were late to school yesterday?"

I nod.

He wipes the tears from his eyes and blows out a breath. "Whoo. Okay. Yes."

I raise an eyebrow. "You know I'll get you back."

"Well, don't try the old 'gluing my underwear fly shut' trick. That won't work. Again."

Rolling my eyes, I shake my head and say, "You just wait." Then, in a quieter voice, I mutter, "I was scared to tell you."

August furrows his brows. "That you're gay? Why?"

"I thought you might not want to hang around with me if you knew."

He looks genuinely hurt. "I'm not prejudiced. I like queer people. After all, I think I might be one."

I shove him, and he shoves me back. And I feel better than I have in a long time.

I blink out of my thoughts as Grandpa continues, "I just want the best for you. Don't miss out on all the romance of life. Your mom has the wrong idea in some regards, but she's right about a few things. Have fun. Don't only work hard."

"We play hard, too, Grandpa. We're training for a triathlon."

He grips my bicep. "Still sounds too serious. Lighten up."

We sit for a moment, watching the program on his television. After a while, I ask, "Am I turning into Mom? Always searching for something that doesn't exist?"

Grandpa's eyes are bright. "No." I let out a relieved breath, but then he adds, "You might be like Lewis, though."

I raise an eyebrow. "How do you mean?"

"He's forever waiting around for your mom to notice him."

"But August notices me." He kisses me now. Even if I'm not sure that's enough.

"True." Grandpa shrugs. "Just make sure to ask for what you want. Now isn't the time to hide."

* * *

I figure there's no better person to ask about this than the horse's mouth, so I call Lewis and meet him on Thursday at my mom's place in Westwood, where he's staying while he's house-sitting for her, which consists mostly of taking in the mail and watering her plants.

Lewis is a tall man with kind eyes, and he's been patiently waiting for my mom to want him as more than a friend for my entire life.

After I help him fill up some watering cans in the backyard and we unroll the hose, I ask, "Why have you never asked my mom out?"

He startles but recovers quickly. "We go out all the time."

"But not as anything other than friends."

"That's true. Not as anything other than friends."

I chew on a cuticle, then shove my hand into my pocket.

"What brought this on?" Lewis asks. "Is it something to do with August?"

"Well," I start. "Um. August and I have been acting like we're more than friends, but I don't think we're boyfriends, and I guess I'm just trying to figure out where I stand with him."

"Can you ask him?"

"Sure. But I'm not sure I want to know the answer." I pause. "Actually, I don't know what I want to ask for. I feel like something is missing, but I don't know what it is."

"You're best friends, and now you have a physical relationship."

I nod. "The beginning of one, at least."

"Well, friendship plus sex doesn't necessarily equal partnership. Is partnership what you want?"

"Kinda? I don't know. I want him in all the ways, but it feels like he's holding something back." I sigh. "It sounds incredibly selfish when I say it out loud. Because I already have so much of him. I guess I'm just not sure that I have him for real."

"Ask him."

"When I know what it is I want to ask him, I will. When I'm not so exhausted from his grueling workouts."

He sets down the watering can. "What are you doing?"

"He and I are training for a triathlon. It's awful."

Lewis perks up. "Really? Can I go out on some rides with you?"

"Why on earth would you want to do that?"

"To get in better shape. I like biking. Swimming and running not so much."

I nod. "Okay. Next time we go biking, I'll give you a heads-up."

"Great."

I don't feel like I've solved anything, but at least I've identified that I want something more, even if I don't know what that is.

* * *

When August comes over in the evening, he knocks on the door, then uses his key to come in, as usual. I've always secretly wondered if his habit of barging in was to see if I was with someone. Not that I dated enough for that to be much of a risk.

I'm ordering tacos for us, and I don't even need to ask him what he wants. He puts a six-pack of beer in the fridge, opens two, handing me one, and sets the caps in the trash.

It's all nice and normal, the way we always are.

Only this time, when we go to the couch to wait for the food to arrive, instead of sitting down next to each other, August presses me into the cushions and settles himself between my legs. "This okay?" he whispers in between kisses.

I nod vigorously. Because this is all I ever wanted. To be able to touch August. To kiss him and have his big body on mine.

Right?

So why do I feel like I'm still missing out on something?

I'm being ridiculous.

We're interrupted by the doorbell ringing, and then we sit at the table and eat our tacos.

August's phone buzzes, and he picks it up and reads an email.

Then he starts scrolling and shows me a GIF that I've never seen before. "Have you ever done this?"

"Superman?"

He nods.

"Um, nope."

"Really?" His look of surprise seems genuine, and I guess, as much as we know about each other's taste in sexual GIFs, maybe we don't really know much about each other—in that respect, at least—at all.

I look to the side. "I haven't actually done that much. I mean, it's just been, um, basic, with the guys I've dated."

"I'm ... Wow. I thought you'd done everything."

"Nope. I guess I haven't really been interested in anyone." He looks at me intently. "Maybe because they weren't you."

When he says things like that, I wonder if maybe his idea of "friends with benefits" is more nuanced than I'd been thinking. So I test the waters. "What are the boundaries here?"

"What do you mean?"

"Do you think this is going to ruin our friendship?"

"No. You're my best friend. You always will be."

"I know."

That's the problem.

The problem is that I want you to be more. I want you to be the love of my life, and I don't know if I can separate out my feelings from the sex. Other people can do that, but I don't think I can.

He must see the conflict in my face, because he sits across from me. "What's the difference between friends and lovers?"

"I don't know," I whisper. "It can't be only sex."

"Well, maybe we can figure it out."

After tacos and kisses and getting comfortably baked, we fall asleep on the couch, tucked into each other.

Exactly as I've always wanted.

CHAPTER 10

August

In the morning, I wake up on the couch with Noah, and it's like I've always been here with him. Maybe because I always have.

Noah's the little spoon, and I've got my arms around him. While part of me wants to stretch, I don't want to disturb how peaceful it is with him curled up against me.

I'm not totally sure why we didn't have sex last night. Maybe because I'm still feeling tentative around him? Maybe because anal does feel like a last frontier? I mean, it's one thing to suck his cock, but it's another to try some of the more acrobatic things we've been teasing each other about for a decade-plus—reverse wheelbarrow or soaring eagle or whatever.

But perhaps I don't have to worry about it right now. There's no rule that says we need to fuck immediately. We can take this a little slower.

Even though I want to jump his bones in pretty much every way.

I have this insistent feeling that I need to treat Noah carefully. He matters to me, and I don't want to fuck this up.

I also don't feel totally confident in the bedroom.

When Noah stirs, I squeeze him, and my heart rate kicks up super fast. He turns to face me, blinking.

"Hey," he says, his voice raspy from sleep.

"Hi." I kiss his nose. I kiss his eyelids. Then I kiss his lips, and soon enough he groans and opens for me. Morning breath doesn't matter to me. I just want to kiss him.

When we break apart, he says, "Um. Good morning," and he gets this shy smile. But then he moves and kind of backs up–slash–falls off the couch, and I try not to laugh too hard.

"You okay?" I ask.

"Yep," he says, standing up, his tone clipped.

"Dos. You're all good." I sit up and tug him to me, my hands on his ass. I'm looking up, and he bends down to kiss me. "Coffee?"

He nods.

And again, I feel like I'm missing something.

* * *

"Noah's acting weird," I tell Shelby at the office later that morning.

"Why do you say that?" Shelby's bleached hair falls in his eyes, and he pushes the strands away.

"I've known him a long time, and he's never acted like this."

"Like what?"

"I dunno."

Shelby sighs and rubs his cheeks.

"What?" I ask. "You know something. Spit it out."

"Have you ever thought that Noah might feel differently about you than you do about him?"

I frown. "What are you talking about?"

"You guys are best friends, right?"

I nod. "Yeah."

"And you've been best friends for how long?"

"Since he moved in next door after his mom took off."

"And, other than those experiments in high school, it's been just friendship between you two all that time. At least, from your perspective."

"Right."

"That's what I'm saying is different for him. He's feeling the opposite of you."

"The opposite of friendship is hate." I know at some level I'm being obtuse, but I don't understand.

Shelby looks exasperated. "No, I don't mean hate. The opposite of *just* friendship is ..." He gives me this significant look, but I have no idea what I'm supposed to be figuring out. There's no way that Noah is ...

In ...

Love ...

With me.

Shit. I swallow hard and stare at Shelby. "How long has that been going on?" I ask quietly.

"I don't know. At least as long as I've worked here."

"No fucking way. You were our first employee."

Shelby raises his eyebrows. "I know what I see."

"But he hasn't acted any differently while we've been partners than he did before then. In law school. College. High school ..."

Has Noah had more feelings for me than I realized, all that time? It seems like it.

"I feel sick," I mutter. "I think I might actually puke."

Shelby leans over and grabs a wastebasket. I hold it tightly, swaying on my feet. I've never fainted before, but I feel like I might.

"Are you sure?" I ask.

"I asked him point-blank, and he admitted he's loved you his entire life."

"Shit."

While my stomach sinks, part of me is elated. Because I've

never had feelings for anyone else. Have my feelings been more than friendly toward Noah?

It's entirely possible.

I slump down in the nearest chair, still holding the trash can. "What the fuck do I do? Should I ask him about it?"

"I mean, as I keep saying to both of you, it's generally good to talk with people."

"Okay." I nod a few times, resolute. "I'll talk with him. But I'm worried if I say the wrong thing, I'll regret it for the rest of my life."

"The only wrong thing that you could say is something that isn't loving. Even as a friend."

"But that's the issue, right? Do I love him as a friend while he loves me as more? And if so, if we stay as friends, will that hurt him? Has he been choosing to be near me, even though I don't return his love?"

The idea makes me heartsick.

I think back on our interactions. Every time I've slung my arm over his shoulders. Every time we've cuddled on the couch. Every time I've kissed his cheek.

Has he been thinking that it's something he wants from a boyfriend, not a best friend?

Have I been hurting him this entire time?

Fuck.

And how many people have known?

"I mean, if you tell him soon and come out as a couple, I win the pool."

"There's a pool?"

Shelby nods. "For years."

"Years?" I ask blankly.

"Years."

"What the actual fuck? How come everyone knew this except me?"

"Because it was one of those kinds of secrets. Everyone *could* know but you."

"But ..." Fuck. I run my hands through my hair.

Noah bustles into the reception area and skids to a stop when he sees me. "Are you okay? Are you sick?"

"I'm fine," I croak. "I just maybe ate something bad. Not sure."

"Are you going to be able to handle the meeting on the Haskell file with Danny? Or do you want to sit it out?"

"I can handle it." I take a deep breath. I need to pull myself together. Work. I need to do my job. I look up. "We need to sort out who is going to interview Johnny's witnesses." We represent a porn star who is suing for sexual harassment.

Shelby smirks. "I know the case is serious, but the witnesses are a bunch of hot porn stars."

Noah shrugs. "They're people."

"Yes ... Gorgeous people who you may or may not have seen naked and in a wide variety of compromising positions."

"Want to come along and take notes?" Noah asks.

Shelby perks up. "Are you serious?"

"It might be helpful to have backup. You're good with people. Maybe you'll see something I don't. Demi can handle the phones until you return."

"I fucking love my job," Shelby mutters, and I'm relieved that things are temporarily back to normal.

I look up at Noah. Is he really in love with me?

And what are my feelings about him? Other than the fact that I want him, I think I've always wanted him, and he's as much my family as my blood relatives.

* * *

If I thought it was a trip sending and receiving porn GIFs with my BFF, it's even weirder sitting across from the man who stars in a good percentage of them. I've met him before, but it never fails to unsettle me at first.

Johnny Haskell, aka Velvet the Cowboy, is imposing in person, probably six foot six or seven. No wonder he has a cock measured in feet. He's just a big guy. His biceps are like bowling balls. He looks like he's a slow talker and a deep thinker, but he's also got this intense dom face when need be. And the sweetest smile and baby cheeks the rest of the time.

No wonder he's a star.

Danny Villaseñor, one of our partners, has been primarily handling his case, but it's starting to get some publicity, and since Noah and I are the faces of the firm, we need to know the specifics.

After we've gotten the pleasantries out of the way and Danny has updated me on the procedural posture of the case, I say, "Tell me everything."

Johnny takes a deep breath. "We got a new director. And this is awkward. Because it's a porn studio, right? So there's a lot of talk about sex." He reddens. "Not just talk. There's a lot of fucking going on. But it's all under contract. We talk about the scenes. They're planned out, at least in broad strokes." He grins at his pun, but then his face falls. "I always talk with the actors about what they're comfortable with. If there's something I should make sure to stay away from. Or something they particularly like."

I can tell how much care he puts into his scenes. He's known for all the eye contact he gives to his partners—at least when they're in a position where he can see their eyes. That's part of what makes him so popular and his scenes so hot.

"I think your costars probably appreciate that."

"I would hope so. I try to treat people the way I want to be treated."

I nod, encouraging him to continue.

"The crew, for the most part, is professional. The founder of the studio was big on ethics and consent. He wanted us to wear condoms. We were always safe. But he had to step away because of an illness, and he left his partner in charge. Business partner, not life partner. Anyway, it started with him wanting us to do a scene that was beyond my costar's limits. I told him no, and he got pissed."

"Then what happened?"

Johnny looks away. Then, in a halting voice, he starts telling us how bad it was.

CHAPTER 11

Noah

That night, when August comes over, he's acting weird. He goes to put the six-pack in the fridge as usual but bangs into the counter with his hip and then fumbles the bottle opener.

"What's up with you?" I finally ask.

"I want to ask you something," August says. He's looking around the room, every direction except at me, and he's shifting his weight from one leg to the other.

"Okay," I say slowly, parsing out the syllables like it's two separate words. "Shoot."

He lets out a loud breath. "At work, I was talking with Shelby, and he said something that I didn't understand. Or, rather, I didn't know whether to believe him or not."

Panic rushes through me, because the only thing that Shelby could have said that would make August act like this is that I have feelings for August. There's nothing going on with the business or any cases. Sure, we have high-stress jobs, but we're used to that.

This, though. This might sink us.

I swallow and nod. "Okay," I say again. This time my voice cracks.

"He said that you're in love with me."

Those words hit like a lead pipe on the floor. I stare at him, and, to my embarrassment, tears well in the corners of my eyes.

I start shaking my head. Not to deny it. But because Shelby kinda betrayed my confidence.

Although I guess he didn't. He figured it out on his own. It was just that August didn't know.

"Is he wrong?" August asks.

"He's not wrong," I say in the tiniest voice. One I haven't used since I was a very small kid. One that says I'm nothing.

"Oh, Noah," August says, and the pity in the words makes me recoil.

I do not want him pitying me.

"It's fine," I say, wiping my eyes and turning away. "It's nothing." I feel like I'm in a bad soap opera. But it's just like August to confront me. He doesn't back down from the hard things. Most of the time, at least.

"I kind of think it's something. How come you never told me?"

"What? And ruin our friendship?"

August shakes his head. "Why would it?"

I stare at him like he's grown horns. "Of course it would. It would ruin everything."

He steps closer, between my legs. His hot breath fans my cheek, and I shudder. "Kissing hasn't ruined everything, has it? And the other stuff we've done."

"No. But it feels like we're playing with fire. Like one wrong move and this is all going to blow up."

August looks insulted. "I'd like to have more faith in us than that."

"You, I have faith in. But I'm not the kind of guy people stick around for."

"Dos. Your grandpa's still around. And your mom leaving had nothing to do with you."

"Except it did," I whisper. "Because if I were enough—"

"No. It's not up to her to decide if you're enough. It's not up to anyone. Because you already are." Another tear slips down my face. "You're scared, aren't you. That's it. You think people you love are going to leave you, so you can't show them that you love them. I'm not leaving you, Noah. Not ever. You're stuck with me forever."

His hands have moved from my face to clutch my waist, then lower, to the front of my shorts. That's not really much of a surprise. August communicates by being physical, and now that we're ... whatever we are ... the times when he might previously have hugged me seem to have turned into something different.

"Is this okay?" He tilts his head toward my groin.

I should say no. Not because I don't want him to touch me. But because I'm so fucking scared of the fallout when this all goes wrong.

I can't seem to stop him, though—mostly because I don't want to. I decide that dealing with the fallout will be a problem for future Noah. Right-now Noah says yes.

Even though current Noah is a little upset that August doesn't seem to return my feelings. He didn't say he loved me back, at any rate.

But best friends with benefits is better than nothing, and if I happen to feel more than he does ... well, that's the way it is.

"Yeah," I whisper. And then I stand there, helpless, as August drops to his knees before me, unbuttons and unzips my shorts, and pulls my dick out of my underwear.

The look on his face as he glances up at me, his whole face happy, his eyes bright but lust-filled, will live rent-free in my brain for the rest of my life.

I run a hand through his hair, loving the curls. He wraps his mouth around my cock without any further preamble.

Oh my gosh, it feels so ... so *good*.

His dark head bobs up and down my dick, and I want to

throw my head back with pleasure but I also want to watch every moment.

"Touch yourself," I whisper. "I want to see you get off."

He grins around my cock, slides his athletic shorts down, and starts jacking himself.

I relax into the pleasure of him sucking my dick while I watch his hand shuttling on his own dick, and the combination is out of this world.

My body tenses, and my orgasm pulses through me in over-whelming waves. I want to stay in this moment and have it never end. At the same time, it's almost unbearable.

He swallows down all of my come, looking up at me, but before he can say anything, I tackle him to the ground, shove his hand to the side, and start sucking him. He smells clean with an undercurrent of musk, and in just a few strokes, he's coming down my throat. I'm grateful to think I might have made him feel anywhere near as good as he made me feel.

But when he's done, I panic. Because instead of talking, we're ... well, definitely not. With one last suck, I pull off of him, and then he's rolling me to my back and kissing the ever-loving stuffing out of me.

I taste both of us in our kiss, and with him on top of me, our wet dicks meet. I groan against him, because I want this. All the time.

He doesn't show any signs of awkwardness, and the way he kisses me is comforting.

August always makes me feel comforted.

He shoves down my shorts and his, then unbuttons my shirt before stripping his off.

"Off. Off," he mutters. "I have to see you naked. I have to feel you."

I grin at him. "Yeah. But I think we went about this backward. Normally you get naked first, *then* have sex."

He shrugs but helps me with the last sleeve of my shirt. He sits back on his heels, his athletic body warm and naked over me, and I'm naked under him.

I feel naked in more ways than one. He's inspecting me. Not to judge me—August accepts me.

But to check me out.

I suck in my stomach, and he laughs. Then he bends down and starts kissing his way up my torso, stopping to lick my nipples, which makes me hiss.

"How have I never connected the dots?" he murmurs. "You've always been hot. And I've always liked being with you. Why did it take so long?"

I want to remind him that we tried in high school, but that would ruin the mood. Especially when he's now kissing my neck and gently sucking on it in a way that's making my dick wonder if it's going to get a second chance here.

I'm both scared that I'm going to mess this up and also wanting so. Much. More. I end up twisting and pushing him so I'm straddling him, my butt over his dick.

We just look at each other. He starts stroking my soft cock, and it hardens, slowly at first, and then ... "Wow," I whisper. "Fuck. I'm ready to go." He's getting hard, too, under my ass.

He grins and tugs me down to kiss him. "We could make this really fun. Want to try any of those positions?"

I blink at him. "For our first time together, you want to do, like, folded deck chair or bulldog?"

He shrugs. "Well, I thought I'd give you the option. But I was thinking that maybe you could ride me."

I inhale sharply. Because I want that. Oh my god, I want that so bad. I nod vigorously, and he laughs.

"But can we do this not on the ground?"

I grin and stand, then reach out a hand to help him up. I expect him to head straight for my bedroom, but instead, he just stands there naked in the living room, kissing me like he has nowhere to go, nothing better to do.

And it makes me feel so cherished, I have tears in my eyes.

Pull yourself together, Noah.

"Let me do this," he whispers. "I want to fuck you, and I want to see what you look like when I'm inside you. Please?"

It's all I can do to nod. I follow him to my room.

CHAPTER 12

August

I t's like a switch flipped. Or a light went on. Noah turns me the fuck on, and I'm realizing that we are completely compatible. I want to worship him.

I'm chastising myself for not figuring this out sooner. We could've been doing this for years.

Years.

And no, I'm not getting ahead of myself because of a couple blowjob sessions. It's *Noah*. The way he looks and smells. The way he sounds. The way he kisses. What he tastes like when he comes.

He's made for me. He's my other half. Plain and simple.

I'm just ... I have to have him, and I haven't ever experienced this sort of single-minded determination before.

He's naked against me, and I walk backward to his bedroom, kissing him the entire way like I can't get enough of him. I can't, of course.

Not really.

He kisses me back as gently or ferociously as I kiss him, and the varied kisses are making me horny.

Horny.

I push him onto the bed and crawl over him, but then I grin down at him.

"Let me see you," I whisper. "Please."

He nods and throws his arms out like he's some kind of human starfish. I scoot to the side and just take him in.

Smooth skin. Defined chest. Because we exercise so much, he's got an athlete's light and lean build.

But his dick. Fuck yes, that thing is gorgeous. He's hard again, and I want him.

What gets me the most, though, are his eyes. Those blue eyes that seem to know all my secrets—and that like me anyway.

Or love me.

I shake my head. I'll process that later.

I find a condom and lube in his nightstand and then stretch out next to him, face to face on our sides, and kiss him.

While we've been close our entire lives, and his body is familiar to me, I've never been able to explore it like this. I get to peek behind the curtain, and I really like that.

I like the way my skin looks next to his, a few shades tanner than him.

I like the feel of him in my mouth when I suck him off.

And I like kissing him.

He's running his hands up and down my arms, and then he pulls me closer. I climb on top of him, because I can't not.

"Let me prep you," I murmur. I'm keeping my voice low because this seems sacred. This seems like something that I need to honor.

"Sure," he whispers.

I give him a smile, and I think his shy smile back likely matches mine.

After several more kisses, I mouth my way down his body to his hip bones. His dick is right there, hard and waiting, but I'm torn. I want to draw this out, but I also want to get to the main event.

Getting to the main event wins, so I suck him as I reach behind and slide my fingers down his crack. When I reach his hole, I press my thumb against it gently, and he moans—the sexiest sound.

After squirting some lube on my fingers, I press one into him, sucking him at the same time.

"God," he groans. "Mes, you're going to be the death of me."

I smile around his cock and finger him, trying to make everything feel as good as it can. He's tight, and I wonder how long it's been since he bottomed. I can't think of the last time he even went on a date.

Not really thoughts I should be having right now, except that knowing that it's been a while for him makes me even hornier.

I love the way Noah tastes—kind of like nothing and kind of like soap or his cologne and kind of like musk. His dick is hard and straining, with a springy head and a notch on the underside. That notch deserves to be played with, so I tongue it, and he moans.

His channel loosens gradually until I can scissor my fingers inside him. No matter what, I do not want to hurt him.

I've done enough of that in the past.

Putting those bad thoughts to the side, I take one big, long suck and then smack his ass gently. "Turn over," I growl.

He snickers. "Okay, sir."

I raise an eyebrow. "To be honest, I kinda liked that."

Laughing, he rolls over onto his belly so his ass is exposed. He helps me spread those taut cheeks so I can get in there, and as I keep prepping him, I enjoy the view.

"You're really fucking hot, Dos."

Noah's head turns, and he strains to look at me over his shoulder. "Yeah?"

I whistle. "I can't wait to get inside you."

He shivers. "Me neither. Come on. I'm ready."

"Okay, hang on." I reach out a hand to hunt down the condom, wherever it landed, but he flips onto his side.

"What are you doing?"

"Looking for the condom."

"Do we need one?" Noah eyes me, and I realize no, we don't fucking need them. He'd tell me if he had any concerns, and I know my last physical results.

"No," I whisper.

"Then fuck me already," he whines, adjusting himself so he's lying on his front again. He humps the mattress a few times, and I laugh and slap his ass.

"Patience."

"No. I've been too fucking patient."

"He swears," I say, delighted.

"Get your fucking dick in me, August Ramirez, before I have to tackle you."

I shrug. "I mean, that could be fun—"

"Stop stalling."

"Okay." I realize I'm shaking. I'm trying to get my hands under control, but my lip is trembling, too.

Noah looks back over his shoulder, and his gaze softens. "Are you okay?"

He sits up and pulls me into a sitting position, too, before climbing into my lap and wrapping his arms and legs around me. Then he holds me while I shudder. "We don't have to," he whispers. "It's not a requirement."

"No," I say. "I want to." My voice drops. "I'm just worried I'm going to be bad at it." *And that by being bad at it, I'll disappoint you. That you've built an image of me in your head that I'm going to destroy by sticking my dick into you.*

"Impossible." He kisses me lightly. Then the kiss gets a little deeper, because I'm reluctant to let go of him. After a moment, he asks, "Do you still want to do it this way? With me on top?"

I nod. Because if he can control what happens, it's less likely that I'm going to do something that would hurt him. Something *else* that would hurt him.

"Okay," he whispers. He reaches under himself to stroke me,

though he needn't bother. I've been pretty much permanently hard since we first kissed at the club on Alice's dare. He grabs the lube and smooths a bit more onto me. It's messy, and he gets some on his leg and my pelvis, but whatever.

His hand stroking me feels so damn good. But then he tilts up and hovers over my dick, positioning my tip at his entrance. Slowly, he sinks down onto me as I watch. The tight heat around my cock threatens to short-circuit my brain.

"Oh, fuck," we both say. He's straining a bit, breathing hard, and I can tell he needs to adjust for a moment.

I hold still, letting him get used to me, even though all I want to do is thrust into him. But after a few moments, the tension in him eases, and his gaze turns lust-filled.

Noah bounces experimentally, and we both groan in pleasure. "Do that again," I murmur, and he nods and complies.

Soon enough, he's riding my cock, and it's not like any porn I've ever seen. Not like any GIF I've sent to him. Because it's not plastic and fake and filtered. He's real, flesh and blood, and he owns me.

He moves up and down a bit faster, and I start thrusting to meet him, and we're both making a lot of noise, and it's so over-whelmingly hot.

"Drill me into the mattress," he says, pulling off.

"Well, okay." I hide my grin with my hand. Once his feet are on the ground and his torso is lying across the bed, his ass at the edge, I get down off the bed, line up, and push inside him again. This time, there's no resistance, no need for him to get used to the stretch. It's just pleasure.

I thrust into him and pull out, again and again and again, and I can tell I'm stimulating his prostate because he tells me so.

The movements raise us up to some higher plane of existence. I want to stay here forever, but I also want the crash of orgasm. I pull us back from the bed a little bit, then reach around and jack Noah's cock, wanting him to come with me.

"You gonna come, Dos?" I grunt out.

"Fucking *yes*," he says, and soon he's clenching and spurting onto my hand, and I can feel the waves rippling through him as he moans. I come soon after, pressing deep into his ass, my dick pumping my release into him. I feel completely like a caveman, and I don't even care. I marked him. He's mine.

I lie on top of him, breathing hard, until my soft dick slips out of him and he sighs in contentment. I kiss his neck, running my hands over him, bracing myself for a review.

I haven't had that many partners in my life, so I don't know that I can compare what it's like being with Noah. All I can say is that I've never felt such a connection to another human being. Noah and I were already connected in that he gets my jokes and I don't have to spell everything out for him. But now we're physically connected, too. With every breath he takes, I feel like we're breathing together. Our flesh merged, and we became one. I don't know what's making me so poetic. I guess because with him, it's special. That's all.

It's not just the sex I like, though.

It's him.

"You good, Dos?" I ask, kissing his shoulder.

"So good," he groans.

I smile against his skin. "Let's clean up and get dinner."

* * *

An hour later, we're lying on the couch like usual, passing a vape back and forth and watching *Lion*.

"That's so scary, to lose your entire family," Noah says, referring to how the little kid in the movie gets on a train and can't find his way back home.

I pull him to me. I'm sated and high and on top of the world. "I'm your family."

"And Grandpa."

"And Grandpa. But you also have the entire Ramirez familia, too." I turn him so he's looking at me. "You know that, right? You and me, we're family."

Noah nods.

"Good." I pull him to my chest, and he nestles his head there. I don't think he's watching the movie anymore, but neither one of us cares.

CHAPTER 13

Noah

Oh my god, I fucked my best friend. And it was everything I ever wanted it to be.

I look over at a sleeping August, his mouth slightly open, curls falling into his face, and I know without a doubt that what we did last night was either the best thing I've ever done—or the worst.

I chide myself. The man I love is in bed with me. I have everything I want. I should be grateful.

August's chest rises and falls, and eventually he stirs. "Hey," he says, his voice morning-hoarse. He gives me a tired smile, and it makes my heart melt.

"Hey." I lean forward and kiss him. He's warm and snuggly, and our legs interlace under the blanket. I move to him like he's a magnet. We've always been this way—August is always affectionate, and I'm always greedy for it. "What do you want to do today?"

August gives me another kiss, then yawns and laughs. "Ugh. I have to do Saturday morning adulting stuff like grocery shopping and getting my oil changed. You?"

I shrug. "I don't know. Maybe I'll ask Lewis if he wants to go for a bike ride."

August blinks. "Without me?"

"He said he wanted to, and I need to do so much more training than you do."

He juts out a lip. "Fair enough. Just come back to me this evening."

I kiss that lip. "You got it."

* * *

Lewis has a truck, so he drives us both to the trailhead. He's a good guy, friendly and solid.

Nice guys finish last, my brain unhelpfully supplies.

I sigh, and he glances over at me. "What's up?"

"It's about August. I told you he and I were, um, fooling around some."

"Yeah..." The "and?" is clear in his voice as he turns onto the road for the national forest.

I slouch in the seat. "You know August has been my best friend since ... forever, and we've shared so much over the years. We have a level of comfort with each other that I've never had with anyone else."

"That's wonderful." Lewis beams at me, then focuses back on the road.

"It's not wonderful. Or rather, it is, but it's all messed up now."

"Why is that?"

"Because we had sex," I mumble. "Not just fooling around."

Lewis is quiet for a moment. "And what does sex mean to you, emotionally?"

"Well, it's a thing you do with your body. It's natural. I don't normally associate that much emotion with it. And with August, it's always been more of a joke than anything else."

"How so?"

"Never mind. It's a silly game we play involving GIFs." I look out the window at the landscape passing by.

"Is having sex with August messing with you?"

"I dunno." I stare. "I think what might be messing with me is that I want all of him, you know? I poured out my heart, but he interpreted it in a way that feels like he's holding something back, even if we've added a physical aspect to our friendship."

"And you want to share everything."

"Yeah." I look over at him. "Am I being too greedy? Is this unrealistic? Should I settle for having sex with my best friend?" Now I'm getting going. "Because most people would ask what I'm complaining about. Don't I have what I want? August, in my life, in my bed." I shake my head. "I just don't feel like we're on the same page with this. It feels like there's something more. Something we're missing."

"You want to give yourself to him and have him accept you. And you want to do the same for him."

"Right. And in a way, we've done that, but something about the label of friend is still throwing me off. Like, why aren't we calling ourselves partners? What's scaring us? Or what's scaring him?"

Lewis pulls into the parking lot and turns off the engine. "I don't know. But what you're experiencing is real and valid. Just because someone else looking in on your life judges you as having nothing to complain about doesn't mean they know a damned thing."

* * *

It's a windy day, which puts me on edge for some reason. Thankfully, once I put on my helmet and get going, following Lewis along the trail, I'm not as affected by the wind, although some dust gets in my face and irritates my eyes under the sunglasses.

Eye irritation. Not tears.

The wind is whipping the foliage, too, and I feel like it's out to get me. I think about how August always holds the tree branches back so I don't get scratched. Lewis doesn't think to do that, and it's probably not possible when we're biking this fast anyway, so I'm pretty sure I'm going to have some scrapes.

Also, after what we did last night, the bike seat is hurting my bottom, but I grit my teeth and bear it as we continue. If I'm going to be having more sex, I'll have to build up some tolerance.

My thighs are about to collapse when we finally reach the top of the hill and look around. Lewis tosses me an energy gel, and even though I think they taste gross, I swallow it down. After I refuel, I go to take a few pictures of the view, but my helmet's in the way, so I loosen it a tad to get the shot. When we start downhill back to the parking lot, I take the lead.

There aren't many hikers on the trail, and I feel some pressure with Lewis behind me, so we're going fast. Honestly, I feel a little out of control. But I can hold on and ride it out to the bottom of the hill. I look up ahead to see where the trail is going and fail to see the small rock right in front of me until I'm almost upon it. Trying to avoid it at the last minute, I overcorrect, and the scenery falls to the side as I go flying—

CHAPTER 14

August

I'm lying on my couch watching junk on YouTube when my phone buzzes with a text from Noah. I grin, thinking it's a porn GIF—not a poorly timed one, but whatever. I squint at his message and frown.

NOAH

Don't worry

I'm being airlifted to UCLA medical center.

My stomach clenches, and my blood runs cold. What? Wait. *What?*

As my vision fuzzes out, I struggle to reread the text. Somehow, with trembling fingers, I start typing, then my muscle memory takes over and my texts come out in a stream of consciousness.

AUGUST

Wait. Are you okay? You're not okay. You're going to the hospital. OMG.

AREYOUOKAY

Holy shit.

I'll meet you there.

What happened

OMG

I'm going to get in my car

Noah, I'm really fucking

Scared

I just want you to be okay

You have to be okay

There's so much I have to tell you.

I'm searching for my shoes, my wallet, my phone.
Wait, my phone is in my hand. I'm a total mess.

I need my keys. I'm out the door and running down the stairs to the garage when I see the three animated dots on the screen indicating that Noah's typing. I hold my breath and stay still, needing to know what he's saying. If he's dying. If this is some kind of joke.

NOAH

I'm going to be okay

I think.

Here's a video. Lewis sent it to me. I'm the one being lifted up.

<attached video>

I'm standing in the stairway watching a forty-three-second video showing a helicopter with a rope hanging below it, hoisting up a man on a body board. It looks scary as fuck.

AUGUST

I'm coming

And you're going to tell me what happened.

I realize I sound bossy, but I'm too scared to care.

Fuck, fuck, *fuck*.

This is too close to what happened to Juli. I remember when we got the call.

There's been an accident.

Your sister's in the hospital.

She may not make it.

I'm swamped by a feeling of helplessness, and I don't know if it's because of Noah or from remembering what it was like with my sister. When I couldn't do anything to save her. To keep her with me.

If she were around now, I'd never let her out of my sight. I'd be driving her everywhere, making sure she was safe. It's ironic, since I barely see my surroundings as I race to my car and start it, peeling out before I even know which way to go. I ask the voice assistant on my phone to look up traffic to the hospital, and I end up doing a sharp U-turn. I really shouldn't be driving. My whole body is shaking, and my brain is racing in circles of worry. I clutch the steering wheel tight because if I didn't, I think I'd break into pieces.

The map program maneuvers me through traffic. One of those idle thoughts comes to me: it doesn't matter whether you're going two miles or twenty, every trip in Los Angeles takes twenty-five minutes. I make it in eighteen by breaking a few laws.

I ditch my car in the parking garage and run to the elevators, which are *so fucking slow* that I give up and take the stairs, leaping down six flights before sprinting to the emergency room entrance.

At the information desk, which is staffed by a tall, thin old man in a candy striper uniform, I pant, "Noah Weston. My partner. He's here."

I'm sure the man thinks I mean domestic partner rather than law partner. If it helps get me in to see Noah, I'll take it.

The volunteer smiles. "Let me look him up. What's your name?"

"August Ramirez."

He starts typing extremely slowly, like he has all the time in the world. I force myself to be patient, but it's tough. Finally, he says, "Ah. He has you down here. He's in room 412. You can wait in the waiting room on the fourth floor. Just take those elevators ..."

I'm on my way to the elevator bank before he finishes talking. I push the button repeatedly, even though I know that won't help. I have to do *something*. When the doors finally open, I get in the lumbering, oversized elevator along with a nurse wearing dark blue scrubs and a janitor pushing a trash can.

I'm so jittery that I'm sure they think I'm abusing controlled substances, but I'm just scared.

Because the love of my life is hurt.

The love.

Of my fucking life.

And Noah doesn't know I love him. He doesn't know that he's the most important part of my whole world. I'd give up every-thing I have if he needed me to. Hell, if he *asked* me to.

I realize that's codependent, and I don't care. I'd do anything for him. He's stood by me through everything—my sister dying, my parents withdrawing into themselves, the guilt of trying to move on with my life, the stress of law school and the bar exam, all the unknowns and fears with starting our business. Every-fucking-thing. Now he's hurt, and I can't stop shaking.

He told me he loves me, which took me by surprise—but also didn't, once I processed it. And I was so out of it in the moment ... and so into him ... I didn't realize I hadn't told him how much he means to me.

It better not be too late, or I'm gonna have a word with the universe.

When the elevator finally gets to the fourth floor, after stopping at every damned floor along the way, I race out and find the nurse's station.

"My boyfriend," I pant, because fuck it, that's what he is. "He's here."

"Okay, honey," she says, giving me a big smile. "What's his name, and we'll find him."

I tell her Noah's name, and she looks up at me again. "You can wait over here," she says, pointing to an area with uncomfortable chairs and a TV playing.

I don't want to sit.

I don't want to watch television.

I want to see Noah.

But I plop my ass down on a chair and put my elbows on my knees and my head in my hands. I need to think. I need to get my breathing under control.

The adrenaline doesn't wear off quickly, though, and I'm still keyed up and anxious five minutes later. Ten. Twenty. I check the clock on the wall and the one on my phone enough times for my battery to start wearing down.

Finally, after what feels like hours, a nurse appears.

"Family of Noah Weston?" he asks.

I pop up like a jack-in-the-box. "Here."

The smile he gives me is the kindest I've ever seen. "Visitors can come in now."

"I can see him?"

"Yes. Follow me."

I hustle down the hospital hallway, with its rails and lights and the smells of disinfectant and humans. Machines beep, and we pass a cart with racks holding meal trays.

When we enter the room, Noah is sleeping propped up in a hospital bed, wrapped in blankets, an IV in the back of his hand and a blood pressure cuff on his arm. His face is covered with cuts and bruises, his nose is bandaged, and half of his hair is shaved, with another bandage over his bare scalp.

Guilt slams into me. Hard.

Noah's injuries are all my fault. I'm the one who pressured him to train for a triathlon he didn't want to do. I'm the one who encourages him to take physical risks.

I burst into tears.

I race to him, resisting the urge to gather him in my arms in case I might hurt him further.

"He looks a little rough, but he's going to be okay," the nurse says.

"What's his diagnosis?"

"We're still running tests, but he hasn't broken any bones. He's pretty scraped up, but only the laceration on his forehead needed stitches. I'll let the doctor talk with you about the rest."

My heart drops.

But Noah's alive, and that's more than we could say for Juli. His breathing is even, and the machines he's hooked up to are all beeping steadily.

I want to wrap him in protective gear and keep him next to me forever.

"Have a seat," the nurse says, dragging a chair over for me. I accept it and sit as close as I can to Noah, gently taking his hand. It's cool, but not cold, and after a moment, Noah blinks those big, beautiful blue eyes and looks at me in confusion.

"Hey," he says. "Where am I?"

"UCLA Medical Center."

"That's right. I knew that. Okay." He looks around. "Do I have a concussion?"

I clear my throat. "I don't know."

"Okay."

He blinks again and seems to fall back asleep, and I study him as he dozes. The doctor comes in and tells me that they're watching him for a concussion but his helmet saved him, and his injuries look worse than they are because of the stitches on his head. His helmet wasn't on tight enough, and it slipped a bit, letting a rock slice him.

I nod and swallow hard. "Thanks."

After the doctor leaves, I watch Noah sleep, his body looking small in the hospital bed. Noah is close to my height, but he's dwarfed by his surroundings. I fix his blanket when he shifts, and then I squirm in the uncomfortable chair until a nurse comes by and checks his vitals. "We're going to have him stay overnight," the nurse tells me, "but he should be able to go home tomorrow."

"Great." My voice sounds scratchy. And apparently I can only say one word at a time. The nurse smiles at me and leaves, and I watch Noah intently.

How could I live without this guy?

I couldn't. I can't fathom a life without him in it. And while I know what I have to say isn't going to fix his head, I can't go any longer without saying it. I run my hands through my hair and start pacing. I'm raw and emotional, but I know what I have to do.

The minutes tick by until Noah wakes up, yawning. "Sorry."

"Don't be." I sit back down, the chair pulled as close as I can get it, and smile at him. "Your color is looking better."

"I'm feeling a little better." He looks at me and clears his throat. "So, I got into a mountain biking accident."

I chuckle without humor. "I can tell. What happened?"

"I fell and hit my head on a rock. Would've been worse if I wasn't wearing a helmet. Would've been better if I hadn't loosened the helmet or gone too fast or gotten distracted."

"Shit," I whisper.

He describes the accident to me—he just lost control going downhill. Luckily he was in front, or Lewis might not have known right away. He was also lucky to be in an area with cell service. Lewis called for help, shot footage of Noah being helicoptered out, and retrieved Noah's bike. It sounds as if Lewis was planning to come to the hospital, but Noah texted him not to. Noah ends by saying, "That life flight was pretty cool."

"I can't believe you were texting *while you were being helicoptered to the hospital*," I say.

Noah lifts his shoulders in an awkward shrug. "I was out of it, but not so out of it I forgot to tell you. Guess some part of me figured you'd want to know."

"Yes," I say forcefully. "I wanted to know." I gulp. "I always want to know what's going on with the love of my life."

He blinks at me and tilts his head. "*What*?"

"I love you," I blurt. "I need you. You scared me, and I can't live without you. I mean, fuck it. We need to be together. Will you marry me, Noah?"

Tears well up in Noah's eyes.

"I'm sorry," I say, holding up my hands, "if that's coming out of left field, but I just can't lose you. I can't lose anyone else."

Noah struggles to sit up, and I can tell he's feeling groggy. "What the hell, August?" He gives me a hard look. "Is this about Juli?"

I shrug. "I mean, maybe. Kinda. I've had enough loss in my life."

"No," he says forcefully. "That's an awful reason to marry someone. What are you even thinking?"

CHAPTER 15

Noah

Anger flares hot in my body, and I know it's not from the drugs or the concussion ... if I even have a concussion.

"What am I *thinking*?" August asks. "I'm thinking I didn't want to let another day go by without telling you that I love you. I'm thinking that I want you by my side, forever. And now I'm wondering what the hell is going on. I thought you loved me. But when I ask you to marry me, you turn me down." He throws up his hands.

"You don't want to marry me," I say, my tone sharp. I don't even bother to keep my voice down. "You're scared of losing me. It's not the same thing."

"I *am* scared to lose you," he mutters. A tear falls from his eye, and it moves my heart. But I'm still upset.

"And that's just it. That's the wrong reason to get married. I don't want to marry you so you can lock me down and keep me from getting hurt. Marrying me won't bring Juli back."

"I know that. But I still want to protect you."

"That's not enough. I've wanted you my entire life, and now that I land in the hospital you suddenly say you love me?" I let out a harsh sigh. "I've wanted to marry you ever since it became a legal possibility—before that, actually. But *now* you ask me?"

"I thought you loved me," he whispers. "Shelby said you did."

"I do fucking love you. I've always loved you!" I yell.

Okay, that was not the way I should have said that. Especially the cussing. I cringe. "I'm sorry," I say more quietly. "I do love you. You're the love of my life, August Ramirez. It's only ever been you for me."

He blinks at me, and it's like he's been physically pushed back. "Wow. And yeah, okay. I love you, too. So you just don't want to get married? That's fine. We don't have to."

I do a facepalm. Which, *ow*. "I *do* want to get married," I say in a steely and determined voice. "And to you. But not like this." I start to gesture, then stop abruptly because there's an IV in my hand. "You want to skip all the steps from being friends to being husbands."

"Plenty of people marry their best friend."

"And *I* want to marry my best friend. But I also want to marry my *boyfriend*. Which you are not."

Wow. I'm being a total jackhole. I should shut up.

"Noah. I don't know how else to tell you that I love you. I want you to be my husband."

"Well, I'm saying no."

"Even though you love me?"

"*Because* I love you," I whisper. For so many years, he's been unaware of my feelings, and now that I get hit on the head, he's all in? Doesn't he understand that he's avoiding the emotional vulnerability of a courtship by going straight to marriage? "Mes, we haven't even dated. How can we get married if we don't even— aren't even with each other like that."

His face falls. "I know we were doing the friends-with-benefits thing, but I thought it had changed. Turned into, you know, more. I kinda thought we were already boyfriends."

"We *are* more, August. But we aren't boyfriends. You're

missing some important territory here. It's like you're on a bullet train going over a bridge from friends to friends with benefits to marriage, but I don't want to do it that quickly. I don't want to skip any parts. The only way I'll marry you is if you walk the territory."

"What do you mean, walk the territory?"

What the hell do I mean? It's a feeling I have, and it's hard to explain. But I do my best. "I mean take a real risk on a real relationship. I'm not marrying you when we haven't done that. We've both been holding back, and I want to make sure we can give each other *everything* first. And I don't mean sex."

August looks utterly dejected. He sits on my bed and holds a hand over my knee, then pulls it back, like he's not sure if he can touch me.

"Hey," I say more gently. "I'm not explaining this well. All I mean is, you're too important to me for us to get married out of fear."

He gives me a weird look. "I've always said that one of the things I like most about you is that you get mad at me."

"I'm not mad at you—" At least, not much.

"But this hasn't made you happy."

"You make me happy," I insist. "I just want everything with you. Marrying you now, without dating, without being boyfriends ... or lovers, won't give it to me."

When it's time for me to be discharged the next day, I don't have to make a call. August is here already. I size him up as he walks into the room. He looks devastatingly handsome, but also just this side of being devastated. I hate that I did that to him.

But I was right yesterday: we can't get married because he's afraid. That'll never work.

"Hey," he says.

"Hey. Thanks for coming."

August nods. He holds up a duffel bag that he's filled with things for me to wear, since I came here in my bike clothes.

He helps me get dressed with gentle hands. I almost don't want him close to me, because I smell bad and I have bandages and bruises all over, but he doesn't seem to give a shit.

"Let me give you a sponge bath," he says. "Clean off some of this dirt and make you feel a little better."

"Can you do it when we get home?" I ask. "I need to get out of here."

"Sure," he says with a nod.

I have to be wheeled out of the hospital in a wheelchair, which makes me feel all kinds of helpless, bad things, but since August is pushing it, it's a little better.

After I sign all the discharge papers and take the care team's instructions, August parks me outside, then goes to get his car and helps me in. I'm sore and awkward, and I don't know what to say.

"August," I start, but he holds up his hand.

"Let's get you home. You have a concussion. You don't need to talk too much."

"Okay," I say quietly.

When we get home, I manage to get out of the car on my own. But August walks behind me up the stairs, and I know it's so he can catch me if I fall. I think I'm touched, but part of me is pissed that it's a legitimate concern.

"Your ass looks biteable," he says, and it makes me laugh.

When we get to my door, he tilts his head. "Do you want to be by yourself? Or should I stick around?"

I want him to stay, but I don't want to ask for it—and because he's my best friend, he sees that and nods and comes in.

"Let's get all the hospital and dirt off of you," he says. "I'll draw you a bath."

Now that I'm home, every part of me aches, and I want to sit on the couch and watch bad TV and wallow. Except no screens for me for a while.

But I follow him to the bathroom, and together we ease off my clothes. I wince as the bandages are exposed, but he's careful. When I'm undressed, he helps me to step into the tub. I sigh as I sit down and close my eyes.

I find that I'm shaking.

"Hey," he says, and he kisses my forehead very softly and gently.

"Don't you be fucking kind to me," I hiss.

"How can I not?"

"Because I rejected you." I throw my hands up, splashing water on him. I hurt all over, and it's making me moody and dramatic. After all, I didn't reject him. I just didn't accept his proposal *yet*.

He wipes it off with a smile. "You aren't now, though, are you?"

I shake my head. I want to sob, but I can hold it back, and I need to stop lashing out at August. It's not his fault I've been in love with him forever and he hasn't given me what I want: the real thing with him.

But I let him wet a washcloth and wash me all over. I let him help me out of the bath and even hand me my toothbrush. I let him dry me off and get me into a big, soft T-shirt and underwear.

And I let him hold my hand and lead me to the couch, where I lie on top of him as usual.

He pets my hair and kisses the top of my head, careful of my injuries. But he doesn't say anything. And that might be the thing that hurts the most. That we're still here for each other. We're in love. Yet we're still so far apart.

Even though we're right on top of one another.

CHAPTER 16

August

Noah says he wants to rest for the remainder of the day. While I don't want to leave him alone—I haven't seen him this listless since his grandmother's funeral, when he was sixteen—I feel like he needs a break from me.

So I drive to the only place besides Noah's house that feels like home: my abuelita's. I go there even though I know I'm going to be smothered by my tías.

In truth, I probably go there *because* I'm going to be smothered by them. It's one of the days when they regularly visit, but we don't have dozens of people over. Abuelita has something delicious cooking on the stove, judging by the spicy aroma in the air, and when I step in the door I instantly feel comforted.

"August!" Tía Rosa comes up and gives me a hug, a glass of rosé in her hand.

"Hey," I say, standing in the living room and looking around awkwardly. "Where's Abuelita?"

"She's taking a nap." Rosa looks me up and down. "Where's Noah?"

I scrub my face. "Um. That's what I wanted to talk with you about. See if you have some advice."

Rosa nods gravely and calls, "Soledad!"

"Sí?" I hear Tía Soledad's voice from the back patio.

"August is here without Noah."

I cringe. "You don't have to announce it."

"Shush," Rosa says. "Is this an emergency?"

Soledad comes running inside. "What emergency? Where is your other half?" she asks, one hand on her hip.

"I have to tell you something," I say, tapping my foot. "Where's Flor?"

"In the kitchen. Flor!" Soledad calls.

"Coming." When she shows up, tottering in her sky-high heels, I hold Rosa's hand and Flor's. Soledad stands in between them. I feel foolish doing this in the middle of the living room, but I wouldn't feel any better anywhere else.

"What's wrong, August?" Rosa asks gently. She squeezes my hand.

I take a deep breath. "I proposed to Noah, and he said no."

They all gasp in unison.

"¡Qué barbaridad!" Soledad says.

"It's awful. It's like a telenovela," Flor says, her eyes wide.

"It's not fucking like a telenovela," I snap. "My life is not a telenovela." I let go of them and slump down on the couch, and Rosa and Flor sit on either side of me, delicately crossing their high-heel-clad legs at the ankles. Soledad perches on the coffee table in front of me.

"August." Flor looks genuinely sympathetic. "I know we've put pressure on you, but it's because we thought it was what you both wanted. I hope Noah knows what he's missing out on, not marrying you."

My stomach clenches. "He said that I was just asking out of fear. Because he was in the hospital."

They all gasp.

"What did you say?"

"What hospital?"

"What's wrong?"

And I realize they don't know the whole story. I open my mouth, and Rosa holds up a finger and scoots out of the room. She returns a moment later with a beer and hands it to me.

I tell them everything. How I got a message from Noah that he was being airlifted and how I realized that I was in love with him for real and wanted to make that formal, but that he said no to my proposal. I know that wasn't the only thing he said, but all I hear when he says "not yet" is "no." I somehow manage to tell them without tearing up, which is a feat, but my chest is tight, and I'm pretty grumpy. "I don't know how to be a good boyfriend. What if I try my hardest and I still let him down?"

When I'm done, Rosa says, "You have to take care of him."

Soledad nods. "You won't let him down. You're in love with him, and he's in love with you."

"He always has been," Flor says. "He just hit his head. Literally. Give him a break." She punches my bicep. "You shouldn't have proposed to him like that. You should do something romantic. Your Noah loves the romance. Don't let your proposal be off the cuff. You have to plan it."

I sigh. "I guess I thought he was a sure bet. So being turned down by the only man I've ever loved is really a kick to the nuts."

They all get heart eyes.

"You care that much about my nuts?" I ask.

"No, cabrón," Flor says. "You said he's the only man you love. That's so romantic."

"Oh, yeah. That." I sip my beer. "He is."

That triggers another round of heart eyes. Rosa crosses her hands over her chest and sighs. Soledad sips her drink, and Flor grins. "How are you going to propose next time?" Flor asks.

I sit back and groan, staring at the ceiling. "I dunno. I'm not. I mean, I don't want to be rejected again."

Rosa says, "You took him by surprise. Maybe he didn't think you really meant it."

"No, he understood. And it felt like he was going to say yes. But he said no."

"Then give him a moment." Soledad nods gravely.

"I don't want to give him a moment. I want him now."

The front door opens, and Tío Raymond walks in. It's cute how devoted they all are to my grandma. My mom's likely coming over, too.

Raymond is smiling at first, but he notices my somber mood.

"Hey," he says, sitting down on a nearby chair after grabbing a Bud Light from the kitchen. "What's going on? How have you been?"

All my aunts look at me.

"Okay, I guess." I shrug.

"Hmm. That was the most morose 'okay' I've ever heard. Is everything all right with you and Noah?"

"Why does everyone assume something's up with me and Noah? I mean, of course you're right. But why couldn't it be the firm? Or something else?"

"Because you're in love with him."

I blink at my uncle. "You knew?"

All my tías nod. They stand up with their glasses. "We're going to check on Abuelita and dinner. You talk with your tío." They disappear into the kitchen, whispering.

Raymond turns to me. "August, you've been in love with Noah since you met," he says gently.

"How did you come to that conclusion way back when?"

He gets a sad look on his face. "I know what love looks like."

I wince, because I don't want to remind him of how he lost his partner in the late 1980s. I don't want to make him relive the horrible things he went through when so many people he knew, so many of his friends, were dying from a mysterious disease for which there was no treatment. When I see historical coverage of the early years of the AIDS epidemic, I want to cry. The world treated us so horribly back then. While plenty of shitty things are going on today—things that Weston & Ramirez tries to combat—I know I'm very lucky.

Then I think about Noah. He and I always say we had it easy. But that's not totally true. "Noah might have some issues about being abandoned," I say. "Since his mom left him with his grandfather."

Raymond nods. "You treat him gently?"

"Of course." I pause. "Well," I add, "I tease him relentlessly, and we prank each other all the time, but he knows it's just in fun."

"Maybe don't prank him so much. That's a childish way to try to get his attention. Instead, let him know you cherish him."

"I do," I whisper, and he raises an eyebrow. "I thought I already was," I amend.

"My advice is, make sure he knows."

I nod.

"You know that life's too short, after what happened with Juli."

"Yeah."

"Since then, you've been willing to try anything. Wild sports. Opening your own law firm. And all that is good ... but sometimes I think you take the wrong risks. You have to live, not pretend that you're living." He gazes at me meaningfully.

"What are you talking about?"

"You don't really get your heart involved."

"I do. I love him."

"Yes, but something's missing."

"Okay. Let me see what I can do."

But I don't know where to start.

* * *

I send around a firm-wide email saying that Noah will be out until he's cleared to return to work. When I walk into the office on

Monday, everyone swarms me to ask how he is, and I do my best to reassure them.

"Noah's going to be okay," I promise, and I think they can tell I mean it. I just don't know if he and I are going to be okay. Or, rather, if we're ever going to be *more* than okay.

After lunch, Shelby jumps in his seat when I walk around the reception desk and take the chair next to him.

"Hey," he says, a hand on his chest. "Are you okay? This must be rough for you, too."

I lean forward and put both my hands on his knees. "Tell me how to fix it."

"Fix ... what? Noah's got good medical care, right? He's just resting and is going to be back at work soon. That's what you said."

I shake my head, and his face falls. "No," I say quickly. "I mean, yes, he's going to be back once the doctor clears him. That's not the problem." I sigh. "The problem's that I love him."

Shelby grins. "That's great!"

"No, it's not."

"Why not? He loves you, too."

"Yeah." I lower my voice. "But I proposed to him in the hospital, and he said no, not yet."

Shelby's jaw drops. "He did what?"

"Don't make me repeat it," I mutter.

"Why wouldn't he say yes?" Shelby murmurs. "That doesn't make sense. He's in love with you. Unless he's against the idea of marriage, but I'd think he would be into it. He seems like the type to want to get married." He raises his hands. "It's not happening for me, but most people seem to want it." He shakes his head slowly, his brow wrinkled. "I don't get it."

"He said we were skipping steps. That I wanted to go from friends to friends with benefits to husbands without being boyfriends."

"Well, to be fair, that sounds accurate. I mean, most people don't just jump into being husbands without some wooing."

"I woo."

Shelby shoves his roller chair back and puts a hand on his hip. "Oh yeah? How?"

I tap my lip. "I bring him dinner."

"That's good. Is that something you used to do when you were just friends?"

"Yeah."

"Then it doesn't count."

"So, what? I have to do different things than we did as friends? I have to be boyfriendy? What's a boyfriendy thing to do?"

"Go on a date. Do you guys ever go on dates?"

"We go out all the time! We go to One. We go hiking. I take him to my abuelita's."

"Hmm. I see the problem. How do you be a boyfriend when what you've been doing forever is pretty much boyfriend stuff, except you've called it friend stuff, so you're all confused?"

"I'm so confused," I agree. "I don't know what to do differently."

"The difference is the vibe, man," Shelby says. "You have to make him feel special."

"I thought I did," I mumble.

He smiles. "Actually, I think you do. But you need to keep doing the things you normally do, except try to do them with more emotion. *Boyfriendy* emotion."

"Boyfriendy emotion." I grimace. "Okay, I have no idea how to do that."

"Think about it."

CHAPTER 17

Noah

Other than briefly visiting his family, August barely leaves my side, working remotely from a laptop at my house, and I feel awful.

Not physically. My body's on the mend. After taking it easy for two days, I can start looking at screens. My bandages get smaller and smaller. My soreness eventually dissipates, and while I've got an ugly gash on my forehead with blue stitches, they tell me it shouldn't leave too big of a scar.

No, I'm feeling horrible because I was too harsh to August in the hospital, and he's acting like it's nothing—like I didn't turn him down. Turn his frigging *marriage proposal* down.

Instead, whenever I wince, he hands me meds and a glass of water, and I thank him quietly. He brings home Viking Pizza, knowing my toppings without asking, and I eat what I can and Venmo him half the total. We get high—don't tell the doctor. I live in gray sweatpants and August's T-shirts that are soft and worn and too big for me ... and that I refuse to take off. We watch *Rogue One* and other Greig Fraser movies. We spend every night tangled in each other's arms, although we attempt nothing more strenuous than hand jobs.

But as my body recovers, my heart is torn.

I should be happy. The man I love wants to marry me. He's taking care of me, and I'm sure once I'm cleared for more vigorous sex, we'll get back to that, too.

He's selfless and here for me and giving me everything I want, and it makes me feel worse and worse. Bad and guilty, like I'm a horrible person. I wonder every time I look at him if I made a mistake. Are my objections to marrying him incorrect or, worse ... unimportant? Is he already who I've always wanted him to be?

Holding him close at night, I wonder if he can tell I'm crying. I don't even know why, except it's all my fault, and I don't know how to fix it.

* * *

Even though I'm not feeling great, I still want to see my grandfather, so August drives me to visit him.

When August and I walk into room 203, though, Grandpa's delusional. He starts talking about how he needs to get home from Louisville and how there's a rat on the ceiling. (It's a security camera.) He doesn't notice that my hair is shaved or that I've got a big bandage on my head. He doesn't even recognize me.

It's hard for me to keep it together, because I want so much to assure him that he'll be okay. Or maybe I want to reassure myself that it's still him inside.

But August holds my hand as we leave, and when we get to his car, he tugs me into his arms without a word. And in so doing, he reminds me why I'm in love with him.

"I wonder whether it's a mistake to go see him on these days," I say, "or if it's the right thing to do. Is it better for him—does he know, on some level, that I'm there, even if he's not having a lucid day? Or is it just upsetting for both of us?"

"I think it's important to you that you see him."

"Maybe."

He gives me a quick kiss and, once I'm settled in the car, takes us home.

"What do you think we should do about his house?" I ask, as we drive down Sunset. When we moved my grandfather to a care facility, we didn't sell his home, the house next door to August's parents'.

"What are you thinking?"

"Well, I could sell it. Or I could move in, although it's inconvenient for work."

August nods.

"We could move in together."

He whips his head around to look at me and then returns his eyes to the traffic. "I have zero objections to living with you, but doing it in the house where you grew up feels like regressing a little, doesn't it?"

"Yeah." I sigh. "I think I need to face facts. Grandpa isn't going to move back in, and I'm trustee of his trust. Maybe I should sell it."

"We could use it a different way. Rent it out. It could be an Airbnb."

"Renting it out to strangers feels wrong. I'd feel like I'm letting go of a part of my history."

"This coming from the man who makes business decisions for our law firm."

"Yeah, I know." We stop at a light, and I gaze at a cluster of tents people are living in. "I wonder if we could use it for something good. Like a charity?"

August squeezes my hand as the light changes and we continue down the boulevard. "That would be a nice thing to do."

"Maybe I could talk to the lobbying group we just took on. They might know someone who could use it."

"I like the way you think, Dos." He studies me for another quick moment. "Looking forward to going back to work?"

"Yeah." I stare out the window at a taco kitchen set up on a corner, quintessential LA.

If only I could look forward to sorting out my confused heart.

* * *

Early that evening, August is putting together something for dinner—in my kitchen; he's barely even visited his own place since I got injured. I'm sitting on the couch in a miserable lump. My phone rings, and it's my mom. I squint at the time. It must be the middle of the night in Italy.

"Hi," I say warily. August hears my tone of voice and comes into the living room, tilting his head to ask whether I want him nearby for moral support.

I nod. I always want him with me. He sits down, pulling me to him, and my phone is loud enough that we can both hear what my mom is saying without putting it on speaker.

"Noah." She sighs dramatically, and my stomach sinks. It's going to be one of *those* conversations. "Can you talk?"

"Um. Sure." August's heart beating under my ear is soothing.

She launches into a tale of woe. Raul, her Italian lover, isn't actually her one true love. She's lost her passport. She's stubbed her toe.

I glance up, and August's rolling his eyes. As usual, I agree with him. While yes, she's my mom, I'm having trouble empathizing with her, because she gets herself into these situations.

"That sucks," I finally say, when she pauses for breath.

August kisses the top of my head. "Tell her," he mutters.

She must hear him, because she says, "Is August there?"

"Yeah. I, uh, got in a bit of an accident and had to go to the hospital."

She gasps. "What?"

"I fell off my bike and got a concussion and some stitches."

Mom makes the appropriate shocked noises that a mom

should, but I'm finding that I don't really want them. Or, rather, they aren't making me feel better.

Then she goes back to her own troubles, and I do my best not to roll my eyes. I don't know why I ever expect things to be different. I'm like a dog getting my hopes up that I'll get taken on a walk. But I never do.

When we hang up, with her promising to come home as soon as she gets her passport sorted out, I throw my phone onto the couch cushion and it bounces to the floor.

August raises an eyebrow.

I sigh.

"Yeah," I say. "I'm going to have to tell her off someday. Or cut her out of my life. Or something. It's just ... it's not that easy, you know?"

"I know, Dos."

"Without her, and with Grandpa in the hospital, you're the only person I have."

He sucks in a sharp breath and moves, sitting forward so he's facing me, one knee on the couch.

I cock my head. "What?"

"I want to talk to you about something. Because what you just said ... you know it's not true, right?"

"What's not true?"

"You think apart from me—not that I'm going anywhere— that you have no one. But it's bullshit. Everyone in the office loves you, Noah. Everyone looks up to you. Our office is a family, too— and not in that toxic way corporations say it, to get people to prioritize their jobs over everything else in their lives. It's a found family that you've had a hand in creating. Shelby's way more than our receptionist. He's my confidant."

"And mine."

"And Danny. Alden. Sam. Charlie. Reyna. Everyone."

I think about the office we've assembled, and yeah. I care about them as individuals, not just in terms of how much revenue they can generate, and I think they care about me, too.

"You can't go thinking I'm all you've got. You have so many people who love you."

I shove his knee. "I'm going to laugh, because I don't want you to make me cry anymore."

He leans forward and kisses me lightly, then kisses each of my eyelids. "If you cry, I will never tell anyone. I keep your secrets. You know this."

I give him a smile, and if it's a little watery, well, so be it. "Yeah, I know."

CHAPTER 18

August

After Noah's been home for a few days—and I've been working from home ... er, his home—he hustles me out of the house, saying that I should go see my family. I ask if he wants to come, but the invitation is halfhearted, because I want to talk with my aunts again.

So, Saturday afternoon is another day at my abuelita's, talking with my trio of tías.

I confide in them over my mom because when I was younger, my mom was always so focused on my younger sisters, but my tías always had time for me. After Juli died, Mom and Dad essentially checked out, and their siblings stepped in to help raise us. Nowadays, Mom is mostly around, but Dad suffered what's called complicated grief. He'd already lost a sister when he was young, and losing a daughter was more than he could cope with. So he's present but not really *present*, even now. Hence my attachment to my tías and Tío Raymond.

I'm sitting in a lawn chair in Abuelita's backyard, holding a beer, while my aunts all sit around a circular glass table, and the topic inevitably turns to Noah not being with me. I sigh. "I wish I could do something to show him that I've changed. That I want him for real. But I already spend all my free time with him, bring him dinner, stuff like that. So the only thing I think I can do is just let him be. Wait for him to change his mind."

"No," Flor says, wagging a finger at me. "You need to make a grand gesture."

I scoff. "What, like in the movies? Go running all over town and show up with a bouquet of flowers? We're not like that."

"You need to tell him that you love him." Rosa nods repeatedly, like this is the answer.

"I already did that. I told him I loved him, and I proposed. In the hospital."

"You need to do it again," Flor says.

"And keep doing it," Soledad adds. "Until he says yes."

"Wear him down. I got it," I say sarcastically. "He's my best friend and maybe my boyfriend. He's not someone I need to torture. He's someone I want to love."

They all pause and get heart eyes.

"You two are meant to be, and that's final," says Soledad. "Mamá!" My grandmother is inside the house doing something.

It doesn't surprise me that they're calling in my grandma. Everyone asks her for advice, although it's usually for cooking or home remedies. When she tells you to put Vicks VapoRub on your feet at night to get rid of a cold, you do it. I still tell people to drink a Mexicoke to cure headaches and stomachaches, and I got that from her.

But love advice?

My grandma appears, sticking her cell phone in her pocket. "Yes?"

"Tell August that he needs to marry Noah." Rosa points at me with her glass and nods gravely.

I roll my eyes.

Abuelita gives me a stern look. "Of course he needs to marry Noah. August knows that. Why haven't you done it?"

"Because he said no." I try not to be exasperated about how many times I've relived that moment. "Or at least not yet."

She smiles knowingly. "Ah, that doesn't mean no. I told your grandfather I would not marry him four times before I finally said yes." She seems incredibly proud of this fact, which I did not know.

"Did you want to marry him?" I ask.

"Of course."

My tías are watching this conversation like it's a tennis match.

"Weren't you scared he would go find someone else?"

"Not if he really loved me." Abuelita shakes her head gravely.

"Wait, say that again," I say.

"If your grandfather really loved me, I knew it wouldn't matter how long it took me to say yes. He wouldn't be going on to the next person."

The light goes on. *This is a test*. On some level, Noah wants to see if I truly love him. Because if I do, I'm not going to go looking for someone else.

What he doesn't realize is that that's basically the life I led while he was dating other people. I've been waiting for him, and I didn't even know it.

But I get it. He wants to be *shown* that I love him. Noah needs *romance*.

My world goes a little sideways. I've never tried to romance my best friend, mostly because, well, he was my best friend. A sure thing. I always knew he'd want to hang out with me.

But he needs me to show him that he means *more*. This isn't about me, but about what *he* needs.

I grin at my grandma. "I understand. I can do that."

I'm picturing all the ways I can ask Noah to marry me.

A surge of energy thrums through me, because I know what I need to do.

He can say no as many times as he needs to until he understands that I'm not proposing due to some sort of obligation—and I'm not going to feel like a stalker, because I know he wants me around. This isn't a situation where I'm ignoring "no means no." I'm just trying to figure out when "not yet" changes to "yes, please."

I fucking love him. He's the sexiest being I've ever met. I want him with a passion I don't have for anything else in my life. And he's my best friend.

That's it. Simple.

My aunts clink their glasses, and my abuelita has a gleam in her eye. "You do understand, don't you, mijo," she says.

"I do. I'm going to act like Abuelo and ask Noah to marry me again and again until he says yes."

"Or until he takes out a restraining order," Rosa says.

"Thanks," I say dryly. "Or that."

After I leave my grandmother's house, I make a few stops before walking into Noah's condo carrying flowers and a box of chocolates. He's sitting on the couch in sweatpants, although he's going to be ready to go back to the office soon.

He looks up. "What's all that?"

"Flowers and chocolates." I stand in front of him.

"Who are they for?"

I look him in the eye. "You."

Noah furrows his brow. I don't blame him. I think the last time I gave him a flower was in sixth grade, when we brought carnations for the whole class. "Um. Valentine's Day is months away."

"I thought that this was one way you show someone you love them." I thrust the flowers into his hand and set the box of See's next to his thigh on the couch.

Noah takes the bouquet, still looking confused. "You're not like this, though. You don't ..." Comprehension dawns on his face. "Oh my god, you're being a *boyfriend*."

I smile and lean down to kiss him. It's a light kiss, although I want to deepen it. "Yeah."

"Then, thanks." He grins, and it was worth the stops to see him look so happy. "I love them. Thank you."

And I love you, dude.

But little does he know this is just the beginning.

When Noah returns to the office the following week, I have Shelby hang a "Welcome back" banner across his door and fill his office with silver and blue balloons.

He walks in to applause from the whole firm, and he looks genuinely moved by how happy everyone is to see him. He gets inundated with hugs and spends several minutes working his way around the assembled group until he gets to me.

"We're really glad you're back," I say. "Me most of all." I give him a hug, because even though I want to kiss him, I want to make sure that we're solid before I do PDA in front of the firm.

But he hugs me back and whispers into my ear, "Thanks for being there for me."

"You're welcome."

Shelby starts clapping, and everyone joins in.

"You're okay, right, Noah?" I ask in his ear.

"I'm better than ever." He smiles.

I whisper, "Do we tell them?"

He looks at all of our friends-coworkers-employees, shrugs, and grins. Then he wraps an arm around my waist and kisses me in front of everyone.

The claps turn into shocked whoops—because not everyone was there at One to see our dare—and cheers.

"Does this mean you two are actually dating?" Danny asks.

"Yeah," Noah says, and I nod.

"I won the pool!" Shelby says. "It didn't count until you two were public." Everyone laughs, while Noah and I shake our heads. I'm trembling a little bit, a combination of excitement and reaction to our being officially and publicly a couple, but it mostly feels freeing.

And maybe like things were always supposed to be this way.

CHAPTER 19

Noah

On my second day back at work, I walk into my office, and there's a box of cupcakes on my desk with a note from August. I scratch the back of my neck and look around. It's not my birthday, and we already celebrated me returning to work. Maybe this is a prank?

I eye the cupcakes suspiciously and open the envelope, half expecting it to be NC-17, but it's just a plain white card that says,

Noah,

I love you.

Marry me?

Love, August.

Goodness gracious, oh my golly gosh. It makes my heart happy that he proposed again, even if I'm not ready to say yes. Because he's not giving up, and truth be told, I don't want him to.

A few minutes later, August pops his head in my door with a hopeful look on his face.

I smile at him but shake my head.

He shrugs and presses his lips together, nodding. I don't want my rejection to hurt him, but I don't want to say yes if I'm not sure.

I tentatively stick a finger in the frosting and lick it off, and his eyes flare.

Also, it really is frosting, not toothpaste or anything.

Then he gets a determined look on his face, and I wonder what the heck is going on. August is one of the most persuasive men I've ever met. Is he not going to stop showing me how much he wants to marry me?

Because ...

Because that might work.

But I need to be sure.

* * *

The next day, I arrive in my office to find August sitting in my chair behind my desk, typing away on my computer. He's wearing his usual white dress shirt and blue tie, and he looks amazing, although I want to retie his tie. He smells good, too. He's so big and muscular that he looks like he owns the place. And, well, he kind of does.

I shrug off my jacket, place it on a hanger on the back of the door, then blurt, "How do you know my password?"

He glances up at me, then goes back to what he's doing. "Shelby."

I roll my eyes. "Okay, that figures. And what on earth are you doing?"

"Proposing. Want to marry me?" He raises both eyebrows and smiles.

I chuckle at how nonchalant he is. "No." *Yes.* "You're impossible." *You're amazing.*

"Okay. I'll get you yet," he says. He stands and gives me a quick peck on the lips, then slides past me. "Gotta go to court."

I stare at him, stunned, and then sit down.

On my desktop is an open Word document that says,
Dear Noah,

Please marry me. You're the love of my life, and I want to show you every day how much you mean to me.

Love, August.

Holy moly. My heart rate picks up, and my skin tingles, and I can't control the smile on my face. It feels like maybe he got the message. And maybe he really does want to be my boyfriend. Or more.

I'm not going to be able to keep saying no, since all I want to do is say yes.

But now I'm curious as to how far he'll go with this.

* * *

I soon find out. The following week, I walk into the lobby and the entire office is standing around, grinning, holding balloons. Some of the balloons spell out "MARRY ME NOAH."

I laugh and shake my head. "Oh my gosh, August. No, I can't. You're ridiculous."

Everyone's shoulders slump—except, for some reason, August looks triumphant.

I don't understand why, but okay. I hug him. "'No' means 'not yet,' okay?" I whisper.

"Yeah, I know," he whispers back, his lips tickling my ear. "I'm going to prove to you that I mean it. When you were in the hospital, I got it wrong. You need romance, and I'm going to give it to you. *Show* you that you mean *everything* to me."

His words make me shiver, and I kiss him.

"I don't get you two," Charlie says, shaking his head and holding the *O* balloon. "August said he's proposed a few times, but he thought this time … It's like you're playing some game of 'Don't get married.'"

"Even though you both want to be," Shelby chimes in.

"I mean, if you didn't want to get married, we'd understand," Sam says. "I don't know if I want to get married."

"But we do," August says.

I nod, feeling warm and fuzzy. "Yeah. We do. Just not yet."

"And this is some sort of *thing*, okay," Shelby says. "Like how you two send each other porn all day."

Danny whips his head around to stare at me and August. "Is *that* what you two are texting when you're acting all sneaky-sneaky?"

While I look sheepish, August shoves his hands into his suit pockets, looks up at the ceiling, and whistles.

"I can't believe you two." Danny starts laughing. "You have so many secrets."

I spread my hands. "We're both kinda stubborn."

"And clueless," says Charlie.

"To what's right in front of you," Danny adds.

"Oh, no. We know," August says, coming up behind me and wrapping me in a hug. He kisses my cheek, and I'm battling between sighing into him and shoving him away.

"Are you going to keep proposing every day until he says yes?" Alden asks, a hopeful look on his face.

August grins and gives me another kiss on the cheek. "I have to keep this one on his toes. So maybe, maybe not. You'll just have to wait and see."

* * *

At lunch with Danny and Alden—August begged off to prepare for an afternoon hearing—Danny looks at me curiously. "So, August has proposed more than once?"

I nod. "A few times."

"And you've said no each time."

I nod again, taking a bite of my turkey sandwich. "Yeah."

"Why?"

"I guess ..." I start. "He's been my best friend for so long that

I'm not sure what this is … this thing where we're in love. It's hard to make the transition from friends to something else."

Except August is trying, and that effort is chipping away at my resistance.

Danny sips his Coke. He's been known to give love life advice on his social media channel. That doesn't mean I'm ready to listen to him, but it also doesn't mean I should ignore him. "What makes you think you can't marry your best friend? What do you think a boyfriend is?"

"Someone who is more—" I trail off.

"More what? More passionate? More into you? More romantic?"

I nod. "Yeah, all of that. A little bit."

"And do you think your boyfriend is going to be that way every single day of your life?" Danny sits back.

"I mean, I guess there's a honeymoon period and then things cool off."

Danny presses his lips together. "Okay, and then what happens?"

"Then you're companions, I guess." I look between him and Alden.

But Danny's one of our best litigators for a reason, and now he's cross-examining me. "Another word for companions who really like each other and possibly love each other is—"

"Best friends." I pinch the bridge of my nose and sigh. "I know I'm being a jerk about this. I guess … I just want to be sure."

Danny shakes his head. "I think you needed it to be proved to you that he wants you the way you want him. That's okay." He lowers his voice. "Is it working? What August is doing?"

"I think I'm getting the point." My heart starts beating faster.

"I think your best friend is the love of your life," Alden says, "and he's in love with his best friend, too."

"And is that enough?" Danny asks me.

I nod. "It is."

* * *

The following week, I'm standing in a darkened room with a laptop projector, giving a presentation, and my phone chimes in my pocket. I grin and keep going with my spiel. I'm sure it's porn. I don't get too flustered, because it only sounds once.

But when I get to my car and check my phone, the message is a video from August.

I click on it.

He's walking down the street to the office, the phone in selfie mode, and wind distorts the audio. But he grins into the camera.

"Noah, I just wanted you to know that you've got this presentation. You'll reel them in. You always do, and you're the absolute best at being the face of our firm. I'm so proud to be your partner." He looks down and smiles, then raises his eyes to the screen again. "I want to be your partner for real, too. I want to tell you every day how much I love you and appreciate you. I'm planning on doing that whether you marry me or not, but I'd like to make it official. Will you marry me, Noah? I love you always."

My heart flutters, and I almost drop the phone.

I want to tell him yes, and I have to say that seeing him try this hard is doing something to me.

It's showing me that he really does want to be more than friends.

And I'm finding it hard to not go to him right now.

* * *

When I get home from work, my condo is illuminated only by a pair of candles on my dining table, which is set for two, a bottle of wine open, and I grin and shake my head.

August walks over to me, all suave and sexy, and before I can take off my jacket, he's down on one knee, holding out a titanium ring.

"Noah Weston, you're the love of my life. Will you marry me?"

I gaze at him, the angular face that I've memorized, with his kind but mischievous dark eyes and his set jaw. "I want to say yes," I whisper. "Keep asking."

"Deal," he says, and winks at me. He stands up and kisses me hard, and I kiss him back.

We don't have dinner for a while, and it ends up a little burned.

I don't care.

* * *

August and I walk through the Grove, holding hands. The outdoor mall is full of shoppers and tourists, so no one is really paying much attention to anyone else.

We've come here many times before, but never since we've known each other so intimately. It feels like we're boyfriends out on the town, not best friends hanging out. Even though he's still my best friend, and my heart is filled to the brim with happiness.

I still haven't said yes to his many proposals, but I know I will.

He knows I will, too.

Now it's a game, but there are only winners when we play.

I lean into him and kiss his cheek. "I fucking love you, you know that?"

"He swears!" he says, kissing me back. "I know." He grins. "Should I ask? Is this where you want me to propose? In front of See's Candies?"

I laugh. "No. And no." He gets down on one knee anyway, and I laugh and shove him. We're attracting a crowd, and he pulls out a ring. I roll my eyes, because of course he's carrying it around.

"He's kidding," I say loudly, although there are a lot of sharp intakes of breath and phones held up.

"No, I'm not," August says with utmost sincerity. "Marry me, Noah."

"Get up here," I say, shaking my head, then lean down and haul him up by his armpits to kiss me.

We get a smattering of applause.

"Are you two getting married?" a girl about six years old asks, holding an American Girl doll.

"No," I say at the same time August says, "Yes."

"Eventually," he adds.

I nod at that, and there's more applause. I grin. He grins.

I love him.

* * *

Now that I'm cleared for sex and feeling much better, we're back at it. We're lying naked in August's bed, fucked out, but it's not enough.

"I don't know if I'll ever get enough of you," I admit.

"Why do you say that?"

"Because I couldn't get enough of you before, when we were just platonic. And now that we're"—I gesture between us—"like this ..."

"Physical. Having sex. Bumping uglies. Playing hide the sausage—" I glare at him, and he cracks up. "Yeah, I get it. Now that our relationship is at a different level."

"I can't seem to stop. I don't *want* to stop. I want to fuck you, August. I want you to take me. I fantasize about you bending me over a desk at work and railing me hard—sweeping all the papers onto the floor and just ... having me."

He shivers. "I am very into this visual. You've sent me GIFs like this. Would I still be in my suit? My pants down just enough to take out my cock and pump your ass full of my come?"

"God. Yes. That. Please."

August smiles against my back. "Consider it done."

"I want to go through every GIF we've ever sent each other and do them all."

He snorts. "Even mutual penetration?"

"I dunno. But, sure, we can try it. So, even that one. Because they sound like they'll be fun. With you."

He studies me, then his face falls.

"What?" I ask.

"All that time we wasted, from me being completely clueless."

"Yeah." I pause. "Well, it's not your fault, first of all. Shelby told me you heard what I said in high school, about not being interested in you. I'm so sorry. It wasn't true. And then, I don't know. Have we really wasted time? We've been with each other every step of the way."

"Maybe. But I've only just realized what you need, and I'm so sorry I blurted out what I did in the hospital. I mean, I'm not sorry I proposed, but I'm sorry I did it in a way that was coming from a place of fear instead of a place of love."

And that's all I ever wanted him to realize. "It's okay. Neither one of us is perfect. I wasted time by not being forthcoming about my feelings to you, by fearing to take that risk. It's nonsensical, because I'm willing to take so many risks for you—even doing things I hate, like a triathlon. Just not that one, for some reason."

"Which one?"

"The one where we fall for each other." I kiss him, and he kisses me back, our legs twined together.

"But now it's finally happened."

CHAPTER 20

August

My grandma was right. I'm not fearing rejection or risk now. I'm on top of the world, paradoxically, since Noah keeps encouraging me.

He says "No, *not yet*." He says no, but then he says, "Keep asking."

He wants me to prove I mean it.

Fine.

I will.

Shelby keeps giving me pitying looks, but he doesn't understand. With each rejection, the bond between Noah and me gets stronger. It means that I'm willing to risk looking foolish for him. And it means he's learning to trust me more and more.

I'm good with that.

I propose to him after we see a band at the Wiltern. Then again, five minutes later, as we're walking past the Bank of Hope at the corner of Western and Olympic. And ten minutes later while seated at our favorite restaurant, on Western, two blocks south of Olympic.

I propose to him at Griffith Park (he should've expected that one; we never go there) and at a funny little art gallery and bookstore called La Luz de Jesus—in the taxidermy section.

Where the hell is he finally going to say yes?

I propose to him in front of a Funko Pop display in a toy shop. I ask him to marry me in front of my aunts. They almost claw him to death when he says no, but he says it with a laugh, and I'm laughing, too, and they just lift up their chins, judging him.

But my abuelita has a gleam in her eyes.

* * *

Besides trying to be a boyfriend by taking Noah out to more places —and not acting platonic when we're there—I think about other ways that I can support him.

So when his mom comes home from Italy, I go with him to see her. As is typical, she didn't invite him over, but she didn't say no when he asked if he could stop by, either.

He fidgets when he walks into her house, like he's remembering what it was like to be a child wanting her approval. She's not cruel, but she's missing something. The gene that puts her son first.

I'll take on that responsibility.

"Mom," Noah says, sucking in a big breath and squaring his shoulders after they exchange pleasantries and we sit down in her living room, "we need to have a discussion about what kind of relationship we're going to have going forward."

She arches a brow. "What are you talking about?"

"I've been thinking about what it was like when you left me with Grandpa because your boyfriend didn't want me around. I was nine, and you abandoned me." His mom opens her mouth to protest, but he keeps going. I'm so proud of him, because ordinarily he'd be polite and let her talk. But he needs to get this off his chest. "But now that I'm an adult, you call me and complain about whoever is treating you bad. I'm your son, not your therapist.

154

You've never given me any emotional support. You just take and take, and normally I have a lot to give. But if you're going to be in my life, we need to create some boundaries of what is okay and what's not. What you can talk about with me, and what you should discuss with a professional or a friend. I don't want to cut off contact entirely, but I also can't keep going on like this, where it's so one-sided. It's dysfunctional, and I'm not going to put up with it anymore. I can't keep wishing you'd be different and then feeling like a failure when you're not."

"Noah," she says, tears in her eyes.

For a while, she doesn't say anything else, and neither does he.

Finally, she says, lip trembling, "I can't even argue with you. I'm sorry. I've been a bad mother."

"Maybe, but we can't go back into the past and change things. That's why I'm talking about what is acceptable now."

She starts sobbing. "This isn't how I wanted things to go with you."

"Then you can show me going forward. For now, though, I'm saying enough is enough." He lets out a breath. "I'm not cutting you out. If August and I get married"—my ears prick up—"you'll be invited."

"Married?"

"We're talking about it."

His mom looks between us. "Okay."

"I'm not going to not invite my own mother to my wedding. But before you contact me in the future, I want you to think about what you're doing. Are you treating me like a son? Or something else?"

She swallows hard.

While I half expect her to start screaming and ranting, she just nods, like she's accepting what he said. Part of me isn't surprised. After how selfish she's acted his entire life, she must've known this was coming eventually.

"Oh, and you should go see Grandpa sometime. Before he

doesn't recognize any of us anymore." Noah stands and looks at me. "Let's go home. See you later, Mom."

She stands and gives him a hug, which he returns. But he doesn't say anything else.

When we get home, Noah beelines to his bed and flops onto it face first, shoes on, head buried in the pillow.

I hover at the doorway, not knowing whether to enter. But fuck it. I slip off my shoes and lie down next to him, tugging him to me.

He traces a pattern on the mattress. "I guess part of me thought she'd fight me more," he whispers. "If she fought me about limiting contact, it'd mean she really wanted me."

My heart breaks for him. "She doesn't deserve you. You were a grown-up and kept your cool and talked about what's bothering you. You set reasonable boundaries, which she's never had before. Be proud of sticking up for yourself. And it's okay to be sad. It's hard to accept that a relationship with your parents is maybe never going to be what you wish it were. You have to grieve."

"I think I'm grieving my grandpa, too. Even though he's still around."

"He's ... not the same as he used to be," I agree.

"Yeah." He continues moving his fingertips over the sheet. "Thanks for being there."

"Always. I will always be here for you," I promise. I scratch my neck. "And I was thinking. Do you want to go to therapy?"

His shoulders stiffen. "For ... this?"

"Well, actually, I was thinking about going to talk to someone about Juli. But you, if you want to talk to someone about your mom, maybe it would help. We could go together, if you like."

Noah nods into the pillow. "Okay. That's a good idea. And thanks again for coming with me today. I know that was an uncomfortable meeting. Part of me wanted to skip it."

I wrap him in my arms and kiss every exposed inch of skin I can find.

After a moment, I ask, "So, what was that about you telling your mom you're getting married?"

"I think I've been oblivious, too," Noah whispers.

"To what?"

"To how much you care about me."

"So is that a yes?"

"No. But it's not a no, either."

CHAPTER 21

Noah

I'm reviewing some deposition transcripts from the Haskell matter when Shelby pages me over the intercom system.

"What is it?" I ask, when I buzz him back. "I'm at my desk. Why didn't you try here first?"

"Oh. Huh. That's weird. August said he couldn't find you. Well, he wanted to talk with you, and he's in his office."

I roll my eyes. What kind of proposal is he cooking up this time?

I grab a legal pad just in case and head down the hallway to his office, which is at the opposite corner from mine. We each have a view of other high-rise buildings in Century City, but his windows look down on a high school football field.

When I get there, August is at his desk. For once, his tie is perfectly tied, and his crisp shirt is ironed and tucked in. He lifts his chin. "Shut the door, and lock it." Many of the firm's offices don't have locking doors, but his and mine do.

I shiver. His command makes me *feel things*, and I do as he says, my cock swelling in anticipation. I think—I hope—I know where this is going.

When he stands up, his slacks clearly show his erection. There's even a wet spot where they're damp from precome.

I give him a cocky grin. "What do you want?"

"I want you to strip. Slowly."

Shit. Are we really doing this?

I look around nervously, but his office has no windows facing into the hallway. And since we're on the fourteenth floor—really the thirteenth—it's not like anyone can look in from outside unless they have a drone.

So ... the heck with it. I keep my eyes locked on his as I lick my lips and slowly take off my tie, sliding it around my collar and draping it over the back of a chair. I slip out of my shoes and get the awkward taking-my-socks-off part over with. He doesn't seem to mind. In fact, judging by his heated expression, he likes me being kind of submissive to him. Or maybe he likes me bending over.

I unbutton my shirt slowly, letting it fall open and expose my undershirt. Then I shuck both off and stand in his office wearing only slacks.

"You're so unbelievably beautiful," August murmurs.

I grin and unfasten my belt, then my button and zipper. And I let my pants slide to the floor, leaving me in only my navy boxer briefs, my erection poking out.

"Take those off, too," he commands.

And gosh, if his tone doesn't make several important places on my body clench in anticipation. I comply, still gazing at him as I shimmy them off. When I'm fully naked, my erect dick bobbing in front of me, I run my hand through my hair and then grip my dick at the base, trying to calm myself.

This is exactly what I wanted. I wanted August to take control of me. I wanted him to order me around.

I want him to use me. Heck, I even want this to hurt.

I want him to lose control.

August prowls toward me, his steps deliberate, his gaze ferocious.

"Fuck, you're hot," I blurt.

He grins. "I always love it when you swear." He kisses me, a deep, claiming kiss. The kind I love. The kind that says, "You're *mine*."

Then he backs me against his desk, reaches around me, and shoves all the papers to the floor.

Exactly like my fantasy.

God. Yes.

Part of this is the fact that it's the middle of the day and anyone could knock on the door and catch us.

Part of this is that I'm with *August*, the love of my life.

He turns me over and trails fingers down my back, making me shiver and moan. "Brace yourself on the desk," he says, and I willingly comply.

When he gets to my ass, he slides his index finger to my hole and presses the pad against it.

"I need to be inside you."

"I'm yours," I pant. These days I've been extra careful about prep, so most of the time, I'm good to go.

He kisses my shoulder and grins against my skin. "You are."

He pulls a packet of lube out of his pocket and tears it open. Then he starts to open me up with one finger while using his other hand, also well lubed, to jack me slowly.

He's possessing me, and this is before he's even inside me. He's barely touched me—only in the most rudimentary way.

He moves to the side just enough so I can see him as he undoes his pants and gets his cock out—just like my favorite GIFs. Then he goes back to fingering me open while rubbing his cock against my ass and playing with my balls.

"Yes," I groan, "I'm ready."

"No, you're not. I'm going to fuck you hard, and you need to be properly prepped."

"Fine." My voice sounds whiny.

He slaps my butt. "Patience."

After he gets another finger in there, I think I'm loose enough. "Just put it in me. I want your dick in me. I want you to fuck me hard and I want it now—"

Before I finish my sentence, I feel his thick cockhead pressing up against my hole. I let out a moan that wouldn't shame Velvet the Cowboy.

He pushes inside insistently, not giving me a chance to adjust —which is what I want.

"I want you to use me," I grit out. "I want you to get your pleasure from bending me over a desk."

"Want me to pound your ass?" His tone is conversational, but he's burrowing into me steadily.

"Yes."

With one more push, he's in all the way, his hips flush with my ass. "Then I'm gonna do it, because you matter to me, and I'll give you whatever you want."

"Take it from me," I groan. I know I'm not totally making sense, and I don't care. "Just use me."

He waits another moment to let me get used to the intrusion. I can feel the fabric of his suit pants against my naked legs, and his tie brushes my back.

"This is hot," he murmurs. "You all bent over and naked, and me inside you. I'm going to fuck you so hard you see stars."

"Please." I'm begging, and I don't care. Begging is fine.

He nods against my skin and leans around to kiss me. I kiss him over my shoulder, and then he starts moving. Really moving. He slides in and out of me, and with every thrust, he adjusts the angle, trying to find the one that works best. When he grazes my prostate, I yelp, and he hisses.

"There. Fucking there," I whisper.

And he stays there, relentless. His cock rubs against my sensitive spot again and again and again. He cradles my dick in his other hand, jacking me in time with his thrusts. He's pounding into me hard, giving me exactly what I wanted.

I wanted to be his whole world. I wanted him to feel for me what I feel for him.

I wanted this to be naughty and hot as heck.

I wanted him to use me.

And he does. He seems almost helpless, his hips snapping into me. I'm going to be sore tomorrow. *Today.* In ten minutes.

I'll be walking funny when this is done. But for now, it's the best thing I've ever felt.

He's going at it so hard, and then he hits a trigger within me, and I'm flying. I come all over his hand and the desk. He thrusts and thrusts until it's almost too much, and then he jerks up into me and I feel his dick pulsing, his hot breath on my neck, the soft fabric of his clothes against my naked skin.

We stay there, him inside me, me spent and still bracing myself against the desk, until he bursts out laughing.

"What?" I ask.

"That was the hottest sex I've ever had in my life, Dos."

"I was worried for a moment."

"Don't be." He kisses me again and then pulls out. I wince.

He reaches for the Kleenex and hands me a wad of tissues. He wipes his dick off, then tucks himself back in and gets to work helping to clean me up.

"We may need to get some Clorox for the furniture," he says.

I laugh. "Yeah, I think so."

As I slide on my underwear, he grips me to him, kissing me hard. "That was unbelievable."

"You made my fantasy come true." My insides are all warm and happy, even if my body will be sore.

"That's one GIF down, how many to go?"

"Many."

August helps me put on my shirt. "And how many of our employees were outside listening to us?" he asks.

"In this office? I'd say more than one."

He chuckles and kisses me again. "Finish getting dressed, then let's clean the rest of this up and I'll take you to lunch."

CHAPTER 22

August

When Noah is healed enough, we start training again, making sure to warm up carefully and choosing reasonable routes and workout lengths.

Soon we're both feeling like we can finish the super-sprint-length triathlon that goes through Century City. It's 400 meters in the high school pool, a 10k bike ride, and then a 2.5k run.

While I was nervous about getting Noah back on a bike, especially since we're going to be using street bikes, we both bought better helmets and protective padding. We look like nerds, but I don't care. We've learned the safety-first lesson.

When the day of the triathlon arrives, we wait in line to get our numbers. Music is playing even though it's not much past dawn, and athletes are milling around everywhere. We'll start in waves.

I'm pumped, but I can see Noah is nervous. He's recovered from his injuries, but he still isn't as into sports as I am. I want to tell him he can back out, no hard feelings, but I know he'd glare at me if I did that. I push him into these things, and he pushes me in business, and that's the way we are.

It's a good thing.

The day is cool, with a gentle breeze blowing, and the air smells like sunscreen and auto exhaust and flowers. It smells like California.

We stretch our muscles, and when it's our turn, we make our way to the edge of the pool. I don't want to do this without Noah, so I decide my personal time doesn't matter. All I want is to finish this thing with him at my side.

When the buzzer goes off and we jump into the pool, I swim as fast as I can, but I also keep looking to see if he's keeping pace.

Thankfully, he is.

We finish our laps and head for our bikes. Before we hop on, I hip check him. "Come on, dude. This is going to be fun."

"No it's not. It's going to be torture."

"But then it'll be over, and there are so many ways I can reward you after," I say.

"And now you're making me think about that, and waiting is more torture."

Shaking and still wet, we get our shoes into the toe clips and take off. Again, I stay with him.

"Don't hang back because of me," he says. "I know you could go faster."

"I want to do this with you." It's not a competition against anyone else. All I want to prove to myself is that I can finish.

But more important, I want to prove to Noah that I'll stay with him always.

The bike race doesn't take that long, and before we know it, we're setting our bikes to the side, changing shoes, and getting ready to run on wobbly legs.

We take off, and this time, I'm struggling to keep up with him. I'm not sure where Noah is getting this second wind, but I'm happy to see it.

I think about how many times I've wheedled him to go along with me, but I wonder if I even needed to. Or if he just liked to be asked.

The way he's liking it when I ask him to marry me.

After all the swimming and biking, the run takes a bit more out of me than I anticipated, but we make it to the finish line, then collapse on a patch of grass nearby.

I look at Noah, who's lying on his back, panting. "Good job," I say.

"I can't believe we finished."

"There's not much we can't do if we do it together."

"Yeah." He gives me a funny little smile. "True."

I roll over onto my stomach and look into his eyes. "Want to marry me now?"

Noah laughs and shakes his head. "No."

"Why do I feel like your 'no' means 'yes'?"

"Normally, 'no' does mean 'no.' In this case? I guess you'll just have to wait and see." Noah trails a finger along my jaw. "Are you ever going to stop asking?"

"Never. Abuelita told me my grandfather proposed to her many times before she said yes."

He blinks. "Really?"

"She wanted to be sure he meant it. That he wasn't just going to go find someone else."

"That's a little icky," Noah says. "Like, what if she really didn't like him, but he kept asking?"

"She must've let him know somehow."

Noah gives me a little smile. "Like I said. Keep asking."

My heart soars, and it's more of an adrenaline high than any of the racing we did today.

CHAPTER 23

Noah

When we get home after the triathlon, we're sweaty and sore, but we shed our clothes and kiss, making our way into the hot shower.

Under the spray, I look at August, really look at him. His mischievous eyes and sexy, curly hair. His hard body and sweet center. Also, that talented cock and sculpted ass.

His support, his friendship, his love.

Does he really want to be my husband? I'm starting to believe that he didn't just propose on a whim, even back at the hospital.

He's asked me so many times over the past weeks and months that it feels almost like a joke. Except the look on his face each time tells me that he's serious. And then there's the story about how his abuelita rejected his grandpa a bunch of times before they got married. Because she wanted to be sure that he was thinking only of her.

For a while, I've been pretty darned sure that August is sincere. No one would risk as much public rejection as he has if they didn't mean it.

And he's been so romantic, too.

Over the years, I developed the habit of thinking that I was in love with him, but he didn't love me back. But that doesn't mean I need to keep doing it. He's here, he's mine, and he's not leaving. And neither am I.

I choose him, and I will always choose him. Just like he's choosing me—and he's always chosen me.

We kiss and kiss under the water, not washing yet, just holding each other close. His dark brown eyes are on me when he pulls back, and he looks at me, then shakes his head. Streams of water trickle down his face, along his jaw, and he's so beautiful.

"What?" I ask.

"I can't believe that this is my life. How come I never realized that you were the one? The one I fit with."

"I'll show you how you fit with me," I mutter.

He laughs, white teeth flashing. "Hey, I'm trying to have a moment here."

I kiss him lightly and grab his firm ass. "I know. I'm just not used to dealing with these good, happy feelings. I keep looking around for when it's going to go bad."

"Maybe you can learn a new way of thinking." He reaches for the body wash and pours some into his hand, then starts lathering me up—across my chest, under my arms, over my shoulders. He has me turn around and his hands go everywhere, and it feels so good.

"Did you mean it?" I ask in a small voice.

"Mean what?"

"That you want to marry me? I know you've said it like a dozen times, but sometimes things need repeating before they sink in."

He's silent for a moment, and I turn around and face him. His face is soft, and his eyes look like they're full of tears—though the water hides them. "Yeah, Noah Weston. I really do want to marry you."

"Then yes," I say.

He blinks, and then his expression turns delighted. "Do you mean that?"

"Absolutely. I love you. I've loved you my entire life, and I want you to be mine. In a heteronormative, official way."

"Ha ha. But yeah," he says, kissing me again. "I want to be able to hold you out to everyone as the one I chose, too. Marriage, to me, means we're bonded in a way beyond being best friends—it's deeper. That's how I want you."

"It's how I want you, too."

We get tangled up for a while after that. When we break apart, I say, "This isn't the most romantic story, getting engaged in the shower. I should've said yes at sunset on the beach. Or I should've asked you."

August shrugs. "I don't know. This feels like us. You knew I'd keep asking until you said yes. I just don't have the ring on me right now." He smiles.

"God, you're the best," I mutter, and take over to wash him. "I'm sorry I put you through the wringer. I should've realized that I have everything I want already, with you."

"That's sweet, Dos." He kisses me yet again.

By this point, I'm very clean and very hard, and now I work on getting him very clean. He's already got the very hard taken care of.

"Shower sex kind of sucks," I say. "Want to take me to bed?"

He nods. We rinse ourselves, dry off, and tumble into bed, the fresh sheets smooth and cool against our heated skin.

Every time I've been with August, I've felt like it was a dream come true, but I also kind of didn't believe it was happening.

This? This I believe is happening.

I grab the lube and hand it to him, turning over onto my belly. With insistent, sexy fingers, he works me open, then pats my hip. "C'mon," he says. "On your back to start."

I flip over again and hold my tired legs up. He pours an enormous amount of lube onto his cock before pressing against my entrance, breaching me slowly, watching my reaction.

I inhale sharply, welcoming the intrusion. Welcoming the brief pain. Welcoming my lover inside me, as close as humanly possible.

When he's in all the way, he lowers himself, his chest pressing against mine, and lies there for a moment, letting me get used to him.

"I love you," I whisper.

"I love you, too." He kisses me, and it feels so intimate to be with him this way. I don't think I'll ever get over it. "You good?"

"I'm good." I wiggle my hips. "Start moving."

"Yeah, yeah." August pulls out, then eases back in, and repeats the move. Each time he does, I welcome him, the slip of his dick into my body sating the ache inside me in a way that only he can. As we really get going, he stays in deeper, thrusting and thrusting, faster and faster, and I reach this space in my head and body where there is nothing but pleasure. Nothing but enjoying the feeling of him in me and over me. I rut into his hand at the same time as he ruts into me, loving every second.

After a while, he asks, "Should we try some of those other positions? Bodyguard? Reverse standing cowboy?"

I laugh. "Just fuck me."

August grins. "Or should we call it 'making love' now?"

"Oh my god, no. Get with the program, Mes."

He pulls out, and I arrange myself on my hands and knees. He enters me again and wraps a hand around my cock.

"Fuck," he whispers. "Fuck, fuck. You'd better come soon. You good?"

I love the way he takes care of me.

"Yeah, I'm gonna come," I say in a strained voice. And then my body tenses and overwhelming pleasure takes over, in my brain, in my dick, in my toes. I climax, pulling him along with me. He slams in and stays there, his cock pulsing inside me.

Then he collapses, pushing me back down on the bed, breathing heavily against my skin.

After a while, his cock slips out of me, and I whimper. "I like you in me and on me," I say. "If I had my way, you'd be like this for a good portion of every day."

He smiles against my shoulder. "When would we get any work done?"

"Oh, we'd get work done. In between getting it on on your desk. Or mine."

August laughs and gets off of me, but before I can turn over to face him, he runs a finger down my back, down down down to my cheeks, and then to my hole.

"Do you know how hot it is to see my come leaking out of you? It's like I've marked you as mine."

"Silly. I've always been yours."

He kisses me wildly. "I felt like every time you rejected me, you wanted me. That I wanted you. That we were meant to be together." He presses his forehead to mine. "There's no one else for me."

"And there's never been anyone else for me. It's always been you. Only you." I bite my lip. "When do you want to get married? And what kind of ceremony? Do we need to figure out vows?" My orgasm haze is turning into a whirlwind of thoughts of wedding logistics.

Before I spiral too far, August turns me over and settles between my legs. "Noah, don't you understand I've already loved you for better and for worse, for richer and for poorer, in sickness and in health, and I will continue to do so?"

Oh, god. He's right.

He held me when I passed the bar and when I cried because my mom was being impossible. We started the firm with nothing and now are talking about adding more attorneys. He stayed by my side and nursed me after my bike accident. He never left me, even when I was saying no.

"I've already vowed myself to you," August says. "The rest is just a formality."

Tears slide down my cheeks, and I don't even try to hide them. "Damn. I've been an ass. You're absolutely right. Fuck, I love you."

"So you swearing means you'll really marry me?"

"Yes, I really will," I whisper, and kiss him.

I kiss him for the good times and bad, for when we were poor college students eating boxed mac and cheese and when we won a huge case and rented a Ferrari to go out and celebrate. For when he had the flu and when we're bursting with health and energy.

August tastes like home to me, and he feels like my other half.

"You're the one I want to be with," I say. "Always." I sniffle. "Because I've always wanted you. I've always loved you. I love how you keep me from getting too stuck in the mud. You push me in ways that I need."

"And you push me," he murmurs, kissing along my neck, his plump lips making goose bumps rise. "We wouldn't be here in these condos without you. We wouldn't have a thriving firm where we get to work with so many friends without you."

"When do we tell the others?"

He groans and starts to sit up. "Let's start with my family and see if we survive that."

I laugh.

CHAPTER 24

August

When I walk into my next family party with Noah at my side, and we're holding hands, all three of my tías shriek.

"Are you going to make an honest man of our August?" Flor asks him.

He chuckles. "My *fiancé* is going to make one of me."

Soledad squeals. "No joke?"

"No joke," I assure her.

"That makes me the happiest person on the planet," Rosa says.

"Pretty sure that's us," I say, and a collective "Aww" arises. "I know you're never going to leave us alone, so just know that I did not propose in any manner that is fit for my relatives to know."

"He was naked," Noah says.

I shove him.

"We don't want to hear it," says Flor. "But was he sweet to you?"

"Yeah, he was."

"Then that's all we need to know." She looks to my other tías. "Now we get to plan the wedding reception."

"Um," I say. "Pretty sure Noah and I get to do that."

"Nope. Our job. You stay out of it."

He looks at me and shrugs. "I honestly don't care. As long as I'm marrying you, the details don't matter much to me."

My tías all get their heart eyes, and Tío Raymond gives us cheerful congratulations. Abuelita looks smug, and my parents congratulate us both.

This is one of my family's bigger gatherings, with most of my relatives in attendance, and we wind through it hand in hand. Normally, when we're at events, we go our separate ways part of the time, but right now I feel closer to him than ever, and I want to hang on to him.

I spent too many years disregarding what was right in front of me. I don't want to do that ever again.

"You can let me go," he whispers after a while.

I squeeze his hand. "I know, but I don't want to."

"Okay," he says, and his cheeks go pink. I'll do everything in my power to keep him happy like that for the rest of his life.

At the end of the party, I ask, "Who else do we need to tell, besides the office? Your grandpa?"

Noah nods. "Let's go see him tomorrow."

The following morning, when we walk into the care facility, we're stopped by one of the nurses.

"Can I talk with you for a moment?" she asks.

"Sure," Noah says, looking worried.

"We've prescribed Mr. Weston a new medication, and it seems to be helping him. Your mom okayed it."

Noah lets out a sigh. "Oh, good. Last time I saw him, he was delusional."

She nods. "Hopefully this should reduce the progression of his MND."

"Major neurocognitive disorder," Noah murmurs to me. "It's the medical term for dementia." He smiles at the nurse. "That's great."

"I thought you'd want to know. He seems much more aware since we've adjusted the prescriptions."

Noah reaches out to take my hand, and his palm is clammy. As we walk down the hall, I pull our clasped hands up and kiss his. "Good news."

"*Such* good news."

When we get to his grandpa's room, Mr. Weston is sitting up, and he smiles when we walk in. "Noah!"

That simple word makes us both relax. Noah bounds over to him. "Hey, Grandpa. How are you?"

Mr. Weston shakes his head. "I think I'm good most days, but then some I don't know."

"Yeah." They look at each other. "The staff told us you're on a new medication. How's that going?"

"I think ... it will be okay."

After tidying a few things around the room, Noah sits down. "So, Grandpa. August and I are getting married."

Mr. Weston's smile is so sweet. While nothing compares to Noah's smile, I can see where he gets it from. "That's wonderful."

"We'll make sure you get an invitation," I say.

"I'd like nothing better."

We stay and chat until Mr. Weston starts to get tired, and Noah seems the most relaxed he's been while visiting his grandfather in quite a while.

As we leave the care facility, a question occurs to me. "Hey," I say. "Where do you want to live? I mean, once we're married."

He cocks his head. "Wow, I hadn't thought about it. I guess because you're always over at my place, or I'm at yours."

"Yours has the better view."

"Want to move in?"

I smile at him. "Yeah. And we can go with whatever business plan your brain dreams up for my unit. Sell it or rent it out or do the Airbnb thing. Whatever."

He kisses me lightly. "Sounds good."

* * *

Noah tells me that we can get married anywhere: in front of the fountains at the Grove. Or in Vegas. He doesn't care.

"We don't really have a particular special place," he says. "Because wherever you are is where I want to be."

I close my eyes. "Oh man, Dos. That's sweet."

"But seriously, where would we go? We mostly hang at our condos. We like hiking, but I'm not going to make all of our guests go somewhere like that. I don't think we need to squeeze everyone into your abuelita's backyard. While we founded the firm, I don't think we should get married there."

I chuckle. "Not if we don't want the 'married to your job' jokes."

"So why don't we give your aunts one of our credit cards and let them figure it out. I'm sure it will be fancy and boozy, and that's good enough for me."

And that's how, a month later, we find ourselves at a wedding venue in a rural area northwest of LA with views of grassy hills and the Pacific Ocean. We asked my tías to keep it simple, but judging by the armloads of flowers everywhere, their idea of simple isn't exactly the same as mine. It all looks lovely, though. Most important to us was not waiting any longer. This place had a cancellation, and here we are, with hastily rented tuxedos and Noah's favorite food truck waiting to serve our guests fusion tacos after the ceremony.

Noah's gone to one room with Shelby to get ready, and I'm hanging out with the guests, fidgeting with my boutonniere and tugging at my collar. I wear suits plenty, but that doesn't mean I like them or that they aren't restrictive. Plus, I'm used to Noah straightening me up—well, straightening *my clothes* up, ha ha. But this will have to do.

A guitarist plays quietly as the guests find their seats. While some of the melodies are more traditional wedding tunes or Spanish guitar, I'm amused to hear a rendition of "Milkshake" by Kelis.

"Hey," Danny says, walking up with Alden. Alden's in a trim suit and looks adorable, and Danny's in a tux, like me. Danny and Shelby are both my and Noah's best men. But Shelby's helping Noah right now, and Danny's going to help me. Danny gives Alden a quick kiss before Alden leaves to go sit with other coworkers in the folding chairs. Danny studies me. "You okay?"

"I'm fine," I reply, and I don't think I'm lying. The nausea is just nerves. Everyone has them on their wedding day. "I'll feel better when this is all buttoned up and I know Noah is mine. Lord knows I've asked him enough times."

"He's going to come out here and say his vows. August, come on. Noah has wanted to marry you his entire life."

I chuckle, but while I know Danny is right, some part of me still has irrational fears.

"Do you trust him?" Danny asks.

I don't have to think about that. "Yes. Absolutely. With everything I am."

"Then that's your answer."

I check my phone for the umpteenth time and see the ceremony is about to start. We'd discussed various possibilities, including both of us walking up the aisle at the same time, but in the end, we liked the idea of him coming to me, since I'd pursued him so long.

Noah's mom is sitting toward the front. Ever since Noah confronted her, she's been subdued and respectful—no drama that she's tried to engage Noah in. She's talking animatedly with Lewis, and he's smiling widely at her.

Maybe, just maybe, she can change for the better.

On her other side sits Noah's grandfather, with a caretaker. He's having a lucid day, and he looks happy.

Soon the last guests are seated, and the music shifts to another tune. And suddenly, there he is, the love of my life, in a slim-cut tuxedo, his hair golden in the late afternoon sunlight.

My knees give out. I always thought that "weak in the knees" was only an expression, but I have to grab Danny's bicep to keep from falling over. My heart bounds out of my chest and races to Noah. And before I can stop myself, I'm ignoring all our plans and following it down the aisle to grab his hand and pull him to me.

Noah bursts out laughing when he sees me, and then it turns into a choked sob, his hand over his mouth. Shelby, who'd been accompanying him, takes a step back to give us some space.

I lean over to whisper in Noah's ear, "Oh my god, I love you."

"I love you, too," he whispers back, and the whole crowd sighs.

"I think they heard us," I murmur conspiratorially. We end up walking together up the aisle after all, hand in hand. It feels right. We're done with any imbalance in our relationship—we're equal partners. I know he loves me. He's confident I love him. The end.

When we make it up to the front, the judge gives us a big smile. We asked her to officiate because we've both appeared in front of her many times and still like her. We face each other, holding each other's hands.

I'm never letting him go.

He gazes at me with so much raw love in his eyes, I can hardly bear it. It's like looking at the sun—bright and irresistible but overwhelming.

The judge says some words about our relationship and then has us recite our vows.

The moment hits me hard. I wasn't kidding when I told Noah we already made these promises to each other. I have loved him for better and worse, richer and poorer, in sickness and in health.

I'll love him forever, and I know he'll love me, too.

We exchange simple rings and make it through the rest of the ceremony, and when the judge says it's time to kiss, I step forward so fast everyone laughs.

But they need to know this man is mine.

We kiss until the claps and laughter turn into whoops, and then we break apart, Noah looking radiant and a little sheepish. I'm sure I look triumphant.

Together, we walk back down the aisle as husbands, and it's the way it always should've been.

* * *

Later, we eat tacos in an open-air tent and mingle with our guests. When we're surrounded by our closest friends, Noah visibly relaxes. Like we've made it through the gauntlet, and now it's just another get-together.

"Congratulations, you two!" Shelby says, and hugs us both.

"Absolutely," Sam says. He's holding hands with his boyfriend, Julian Hill, and there's no doubt that my entire family is starstruck. But that takes the heat off of me, so I'm good with it.

Jules, for his part, is gracious, shaking our hands and congratulating us.

"Are either of you going to change your names?" Danny asks, his arm slung around Alden. Those two never seem to be far apart, and it's clear that Danny will do anything for Alden.

"No," I say automatically, and then I realize it's not something we've ever discussed. I look at Noah. "I mean—we'll do whatever you want. If you want to change. If you want me to change. If you want us both to change. But I kind of like Weston & Ramirez."

"Me, too." He smiles, and I resist the urge to kiss him only because we've kissed so often since the ceremony that people are starting to laugh at us. Not that that will stop us for long.

"So. Shelby." I grin. "Do I need to start a pool on when you'll find the love of your life?"

He shakes his head. "Nope. I have, um, someone."

I blink. "You do?"

"Yeah. I just started seeing him." He shifts his weight from foot to foot. "I didn't want to take him out to see all you guys yet. He's a talent agent."

"Well, bring him around to happy hour."

"We'll see."

"Like that's not suspicious," I mutter.

When it's time to dance, Jules steps forward with his usual quiet grace and sings stripped-down versions of some of his biggest love songs for us. It's a lovely surprise, and I make a note to thank both him and Sam later.

We sway together, feeling the truth of Jules's lyrics fill our hearts, and soon others join us, until everyone is dancing.

"Next to the day I met you and the day you agreed to marry me, this is the best day of my life," I tell my husband.

"Same."

* * *

Late that night, Noah and I stumble into our suite at a nearby B and B run by a gay couple Sam knows. They gave us a knowing look when we checked in and promised we'd have the place to ourselves until breakfast tomorrow.

The place is cute, but I couldn't care less about the decor. "It's our wedding night," I say, grinning against Noah's lips.

He kisses me back. "Are you going to deflower me?"

"Such a smartass." I roll my eyes. "Why did I marry you?"

"Because you're desperately in love with me?"

"I am." I have no desire to deny it. "It's always been you. I just didn't think I had a chance with you after hearing you tell Kane that you didn't like me like that. Since you never lie, I took you at your word."

"Yeah," Noah says. "I try not to lie, but that was an unfortunate one." His face falls. "I know the time since then wasn't wasted, because we were always together in some way, but I'm sorry I hurt you and made you feel unwanted."

I grip his jaw and make him look at me. "Everything we did brought us to this point, and I'm pretty happy about where we are right now. I'm not regretting anything, because I have you. Right?"

"Yeah. You do."

I can tell he wants to say more—and I do understand how he's feeling—but I refuse to let our past taint this perfect day. "Less talking, more fucking," I growl, and he laughs.

"Sounds like a plan."

I strip him slowly, starting with his tuxedo jacket and bow tie, then taking off his shirt, one button at a time. I could rush this, but I don't feel like it. We have the rest of our lives to be together. We don't have to speed past any milestone.

Once I get to bare skin—at least on top—things get even better. I love the way he smells. I love how he makes me feel. As I kiss from his neck and shoulder to his deltoid and then along his collarbone, he tilts his head back and groans.

"Dang, Mes. You always make me feel good."

"I intend to keep doing that." I shimmy out of my clothes. "God, I love you."

He snuggles into me, and what was promising to be a hot and heavy session becomes something softer and sweeter and quieter.

It becomes noses pressed to each other and tongues sliding, sipping each other's sweetness. It becomes hands caressing and then cajoling and then sensuous squeezes and rubbing and ... "Hey," I say quietly. "When did you first fall in love with me?"

He closes his eyes. "I'm not sure how old we were, but I know what you did. My mom had *another* new boyfriend, and I was upset. And somehow you knew, but you didn't make me talk about it. You just made me feel better." He smiles. "You made me feel like it was okay to be myself. I wanted to be with you for the rest of my life, because you made me feel cherished."

"I hope I always will." I fumble for my pants, pull out my phone, and start scrolling. "Now, which of these positions do you want to start with?"

"All of them."

I'm standing in front of my grandfather's house next to my husband of two years. I reach over and surreptitiously fix a button he missed on his shirt.

He grins at me.

Our friends, colleagues, members of the community, and the charitable arm of my favorite LGBTQIA+ lobbying group—and client—are all here for the ribbon cutting.

Weston & Ramirez House has its grand opening today. My childhood home is going to be a safe place for teens—especially queer teens—to come when they don't know where to go. We're staffing it with counselors and social workers, plus volunteers who will help the kids develop whatever it is they love to do. August's family is in attendance, and his parents signed up as volunteers.

I couldn't think of a better purpose for one of the only places I ever felt safe when I was young.

After we cut the ribbon, I'm supposed to give a speech about this place's purpose and inspiration, but before I open my mouth, I see August typing on his phone.

A moment later, my phone buzzes in my pocket, and I look at him and laugh.

Then I launch into my spiel.

* * *

Later that day, we go out for a run in our neighborhood. Sweat beads on August's face, and he's taken off his shirt. I'm trying not to admire him too much, but it's difficult, because he's so beautiful.

He's the love of my life. And I'm not afraid to tell him anymore. He's not afraid to tell me how much he loves me, either.

I'm also not afraid of taking risks with him—of any kind. Business, physical, emotional. Sure, some of them might not work out. But if I don't try, I'll miss out on all the possibilities.

It's like that Anais Nin poem. I may have waited too long, but I think I've finally blossomed.

We turn the corner, and I keep up with August easily.

I like this.

I like pushing ourselves to do better. I like being able to be more as part of a couple than I am by myself.

"So, I was thinking," I say, panting a bit.

"What about?"

"I made reservations to go do something. If you want to come with me."

"Sure."

"You don't even know what it is."

"Well, I'll do anything you want, so that's simple. Besides, knowing you, it's probably something like a sunset cruise."

Nope. I grin. "Skydiving."

August stops in the middle of the sidewalk. "What the fuck?"

"I just thought that you shouldn't have to push me so much and that we should go do some things that are a little more challenging."

"You risk-taker, you," he says admiringly.

"You're the one who taught me to trust my body. Certain bike riding mishaps notwithstanding."

"You don't have to do this," he says. "We don't have to do anything extreme."

I look at the ground. "I guess I wanted to show you that I'm willing to take a risk."

"Well, then." August smiles. "Let's do it. Anything else? Another triathlon?"

"I need to train more," I say. "I don't think I'm ready for Ironman yet."

"We don't have to do it this year," he assures me.

I stare at him. "Who are you, and what have you done with August Ramirez? The August Ramirez I know would be charging hard, wanting to mow down everyone in his path so he could be number one at this. Or at least say that he did it, since we're not professional athletes. The August I know has ambitions beyond the normal."

"I still have those ambitions. But I want to do this on our terms. I don't want you getting hurt. I'd rather have you safe."

"Again, you have the biggest sense of adventure of anyone I know, with no sense of self-preservation. I have no idea who you are right now."

"I guess I'm learning that there are consequences to actions."

"Um, you learned that in high school when you swapped out my Vans for a smaller size and I couldn't figure out what was wrong. Until I did and got you back."

August laughs. "No prank this time. I just want to do what we both want to do."

"Then I want to do everything. With you."

* * *

Thank you so much for reading my "sweet, silly boys." Please don't forget to leave a review! Reviews really help readers find books.

If you want to find out whether Noah and August ever tried DP, you can read the bonus scene here: https://BookHip.com/NMDKFWC

Acknowledgments

If you read the scene where Noah sends texts from the hospital and thought, that couldn't happen in real life ... well, it did. It's a very scary feeling to receive a text that says, *here's a video of a life flight with me on a body board*. I'm so glad Garcia, my husband's BFF, is all right.

Thank you to my early readers for your input and guidance: Martin Aguilera, Deb Markanton, Mary Carr, Megan Dischinger, Katy Cuthbertson, Julia Heudorf, and Kristy Lin Billuni. Thank you to my proofreaders: Virginia Tesi Carey and Jerica MacMillan.

Thank you to my editor, Alicia Z. Ramos, for your utter care with the "sweet, silly boys" in my stories.

Thank you to Cory Stierley for taking the cover photo of Mikey. Mikey walked into the shoot with those pants (or rather, the full shiny, paisley suit), and Cory and I loved it. Thanks to Garrett Leigh for designing the cover.

Thank you to J.E. Birk, Rachel Ember, Lex Martin, and Heather Roberts for support. Thank you to my family, as always. Thank you to you, reader, for reading this story.

The Sun and the Moon (audio narrated by Tor Thom and Charley Ongel)

The Stars in the Sky

All the Waters of the Earth

The Ground Beneath Our Feet (audio narrated by Tor Thom and Charley Ongel)

Love in Translation series

Sol

Sombra

Standalone novella

Lumbersexual (audio narrated by Tor Thom and Charley Ongel)

About the Author

Leslie McAdam is a California girl who loves romance and well-defined abs. She lives in a drafty old farmhouse on a small orange tree farm in Southern California with her husband and two children. Leslie's first published book, *The Sun and the Moon*, won a 2015 Watty, which is the world's largest online writing competition. She's gone on to receive additional literary awards and has been featured in multiple publications, including Cosmopolitan.com. Her books have been Top 100 Bestsellers on both Amazon and Apple Books. Leslie is employed by day but spends her nights writing about the men of your fantasies.

Website: https://www.lesliemcadamauthor.com

M/M-only newsletter: http://eepurl.com/hD9a4r

www.ingramcontent.com/pod-product-compliance
Lightning Source LLC
Chambersburg PA
CBHW051527150726
47997CB00001B/420